THE RIVER OF GOLD

Captain Hill glanced at the wiry, appealing Irishman appraisingly. The man named Callaghen.

"You know something about minerals, then,
Callaghen?"

"A little. Most of that I learned in Asia."

"You should spend some time in the desert. There
are all sorts of rumors, Callaghen. Some say there
are vast deposits of gold and silver right here in
the Mohave. Have you heard of the river of gold?
They say it runs through a cave under the
desert . . ."

LOUIS L'AMOUR
CALLAGHEN

BANTAM BOOKS · TORONTO · NEW YORK · LONDON

CALLAGHEN

A Bantam Book | February 1972
17 printings through June 1981

Photograph of Louis L'Amour
by John Hamilton—Globe Photos, Inc.

ISBN 0–553–20265–0

Published simultaneously in the United States and Canada

Bantam Books are published by Bantam Books, Inc. Its trade-
mark, consisting of the words "Bantam Books" and the por-
trayal of a bantam, is Registered in U.S. Patent and Trademark
Office and in other countries. Marca Registrada. Bantam
Books, Inc., 666 Fifth Avenue, New York, New York 10103.

PRINTED IN THE UNITED STATES OF AMERICA

26 25 24 23 22 21 20 19 18 17

To all
who travel the desert road,
wherever the desert,
whatever the time.

CALLAGHEN

CHAPTER 1

Behind the rocks the Mohaves lay waiting—and in the sky, the buzzards. Each was sure of their prey.

The four men lay in a flat place, and the sun was high. Two days had passed without water, four days without food, and their ammunition was down to its last few cartridges.

Before them was a peak they believed to be Eagle Mountain; if so, there was a water hole up the draw to the right. Of this they could not be sure, but they believed in it as a dying man believes in God.

For three days they had thought of that water, longed for it, dreamed wild dreams of it. The most gorgeous woman under heaven would have been spurned by any one of them for one swallow of water, be it brackish, sulphurous, or whatever.

The patrol began as they always begin; in this case there were six enlisted men and one officer. The officer was a proud, honorable, and decent young man with his first command, his first patrol into enemy country, where they had seen no enemies for two whole days and nights.

A camping spot had been decreed, and when the Delaware advised against it the lieutenant felt he could not permit his decision to be questioned. A few miles farther along, the Delaware assured him, there was a water hole and a defensible position. The young lieutenant hesitated, then decided to stay where they were.

They bedded down on level ground, in soft sand. The men slept well, for they were tired. Callaghen was to stand watch the first few hours, to be relieved by Private Baldwin.

1

The night was very clear, and as always in the desert it was cool, almost cold. The heat of the day vanished with the sun, for the rocks and sand did not hold the heat, but surrendered it quickly to the night.

Callaghen was wary. He was an experienced soldier, and he did not like the feel of the night, and he had been watching the Delaware.

The eastern Indian came of a tribe that numbered great trackers and warriors among them, but they had been driven from their homeland and were now scattered widely over the West. The Delaware had seemed uneasy, his head constantly turning, his eyes busy.

The attack came with the first light. Their horses were stampeded, one man was killed, another wounded.

Although the just awakening soldiers got off a few shots, there was no indication they had hit anything. The Indians vanished as they had come, fading into the sands like ghosts.

What followed was sheer hell. After waiting until the sun was up, the lieutenant formed them into a column of twos and they started out. The lieutenant walked beside Callaghen.

"Well, they got what they wanted," he commented, "but it is good to be rid of them."

"If we are."

"You do not think they have gone?"

"No, sir."

"Then why don't they attack?"

Callaghen shrugged. "It is not their way, sir. They are watching us from out there, to see what we will do. They know this desert. They know what is ahead and we do not. They can plan, but our reaction must depend on circumstances."

"You are an educated man," the lieutenant said.

"Possibly. I have never been sure just what the term implies."

The lieutenant glanced at him, but was silent. They plodded on through ankle-deep sand. The dust rose, covering their clothing, their faces and hands. The wounded man kept up. He had been an Indian-fighting soldier for a long time, and he knew what it would mean to fall behind.

The heat was stifling, and there were no clouds. Rocky ridges, bare of vegetation, lay to the left and right, but not close by. Occasionally there were scattered clusters of rock, some greasewood, and clumps of cactus or coarse gray shrubs.

At noon the lieutenant called a brief halt. They ate a little jerked beef and a few pieces of hardtack, and took a swallow of water.

"Sir? If the Lieutenant will permit?"

"What is it, Callaghen?"

"There's a long stretch of sand ahead, wide-open country. Off on the right there are some rocks. I suggest that we take shelter there until the sun goes down. I believe they plan to surround us out in the open, where the sun can do their work for them."

The idea appealed to the lieutenant, and he had ignored one bit of advice to their cost. "All right," he said, "until the sun goes down. We will march farther and faster when it is cool."

Their approach to the rocks was wary, but they arrived safely. The bare rocks were dark red and black, with streaks of quartz through them. It was an isolated cluster, not likely to be chosen by Indians, who prefer a place that can be approached or left under cover.

Once in the shade, the men sat down, took off their hats, and put their heads back. The lieutenant started to take a drink, then saw that the others did not do so. Reluctantly he put his canteen down, for he could not permit them to think he had less endurance than they had.

Callaghen watched the country around them, but the surrounding sand showed nothing. The Delaware, a soft-walking man, came up beside him. "He listened to you," he said. "I hope he will continue to do so."

"Do you know where we are?"

"If that is Eagle Mountain, I do, and I am quite sure that it is. The lieutenant was exploring, you know."

"You speak good English," Callaghen said.

"I went to a good school for five years, and I listen.

I was scouting in Texas with Colonel Sibley and Lieutenant Robert E. Lee."

They did not talk any more, for their mouths were dry. The water in their canteens would soon be gone, and Eagle Mountain lay far off on the horizon.

With the first coolness, they started on. Occasionally the soft sand gave way to harder surface, sometimes to scattered rocks over a hard-packed sand-and-gravel floor.

Refreshed by their rest and by the coolness of the air, the men marched well. When an hour had passed and darkness was closing down on them, some had begun to straggle. The lieutenant paused. "Close up now!" he said. He spoke quietly, but his voice carried. "Keep it closed up."

Presently they took a ten-minute break. The stars appeared, and they walked on, guided by them.

"The Mohaves are like the Apaches," the Delaware said. "They do not like to fight at night. The Comanches, they like it better at night."

Wary of the rock walls now closing in, they made dry camp. The Delaware scouted for water, but found none. They slept fitfully through the night until the sky grew gray. Callaghen was the first man awake, in time to see an Indian ghosting from one rock to another.

He touched the lieutenant. "Sir," he said, "they are closing in."

The last few stars still hung in the sky, and it was still cool. "We can march," the lieutenant said. "All right, men, let's go."

They started, and no shots were fired. Callaghen looked toward the horizon. It was going to be a brutal day.

A mile . . . two miles. Ahead of them lay an apparently wide-open area of sand and scattered brush. Occasionally they saw a Joshua tree stretching its weird twisted arms.

Another mile . . . Every yard covered was to their advantage, but the Mohaves were out there, and the Mohaves knew how long it was since they had stopped at a waterhole, they knew how little water they must have left, and they would know about the wounded man.

The post, if such it could be called, was three days' ride to the southeast. On foot, and under good conditions, it was four to five days, but without adequate water this might stretch from another day to never.

When the attack came it was completely unexpected. It came from a cluster of scattered low rocks that seemed to offer no substantial cover.

The first shot caught the lieutenant in the chest and he fell to his knees coughing. Automatically every man dropped to one knee and returned the fire.

There was no answering fire. The Mohaves had vanished.

"Got my canteen," the man named Baldwin said. "Damn it to hell, they split it!"

"They nicked mine," the Delaware said. "I think that was what they wanted to do."

Callaghen held a canteen to the lieutenant's lips, but he brushed it away. "You will need that, Callaghen. You are in command now."

He put a hand out to the Delaware. "I am sorry. I was wrong not to listen to you."

Callaghen looked around slowly, studying the terrain. There was nothing he could do for the lieutenant. Even if they had been at the fort, he would have died. He knew by the color of the blood and the froth on his lips. The bullet, of heavy caliber, had gone in under his left arm and through his lungs, cutting an artery in transit. He knew the lieutenant was going to die, and the lieutenant knew it too. . . . He died quickly.

The Delaware crawled up beside Callaghen. "They have gone, I think. They want to kill us all, but they do not want to lose even one of their own."

"We have four canteens, five men. We will need water before anything else."

They rolled the body of their officer into a shallow place and scooped sand over him. Callaghen mentally took note of what landmarks there were, and they started on. No shot came, no Indian appeared.

Callaghen now had the lieutenant's pistol and thirty-two rounds of ammunition. He had also taken his papers, money, and whatever else was of value. These must be returned to the post, not only so that the lieutenant's relatives might have them, but so the Indians might not get them.

The sun appeared over the mountains, and already they could feel its heat. Callaghen mentally measured the distance to the mountain toward which he was aiming. It was far, much too far.

The surface was firm for a change. There were scattered, fist-sized rocks, and there was more brush, but none of it was more than knee-high.

He led the way, holding his stride to easy, measured steps. There was no cover near them now, neither shelter for an enemy nor for themselves.

Suddenly he saw two riders off to the left. He recognized his own horse, and swore softly. On the other side were two more riders, who made no attempt to draw closer. They did not fire, and they remained well beyond shooting range.

At ten o'clock Callaghen stopped the men. It was in the middle of a broad, open area, but they were ready to drop with weariness.

He nodded off to their right. "See that bunch of rocks?" he said. "We can make them by noon, and we can find shade there, enough to sit out the day."

Nobody spoke. Their faces showed their extreme fatigue. Croker, the wounded man, was bearing up well. Callaghen went to him. "Don't worry," Croker said, "when you get there, I'll be with you."

After a few minutes Callaghen got them on their feet and started on once more. He held his course straight ahead as if to bypass the rocks, then when not more than two hundred yards from them he suddenly flanked his men. "All right!" he said sharply. "On the double!"

He knew they were ready to drop. He also knew that if the Mohaves guessed his intention they would ride to head him off. He could only hope his line of march would deceive them until the last moment.

They ran, and for men half-dead from heat, exhaustion, and thirst, they ran well. Each man knew it was his own life that was at stake, his own life for which he ran.

Shots rang out, a man stumbled, ran on, then fell.

The Delaware was about to stop but Callaghen waved him on. "Into the rocks!" he commanded.

He dropped to one knee, aimed at a rider, and fired. The Mohave pulled up sharply and swung his horse, hanging far over. The others veered off, and he walked to the fallen man. It was Baldwin, and he was dead.

Stripping him of his ammunition, rifle and almost empty canteen, Callaghen straightened up and began to walk. The others were just reaching the rocks, where there was shelter.

They had found a little shade. The Delaware had crossed to the far side, taking up a half-shaded position from which he could watch. Croker also had found a good firing position.

Sweat dripped down Callaghen's face. He was surprised there was so much moisture left in his parched body, for his lips were cracked, and his eyes smarted from sunburned rims. He put a fresh pebble in his mouth, but it produced little saliva in his dry mouth.

One by one he studied the men as they rested. That they had come so far was a marvel, but they must still move on. If there was water near Eagle Mountain, as the Delaware believed, they would wait there, refresh themselves, and then set out again.

Callaghen knew what he hoped the Indians did not know: that there was no relief. There were no other soldiers to come looking for them; and in all that vast wasteland of the Mohave Desert there was no one from whom they could expect help.

At Camp Cady, when they had ridden out on their patrol—a patrol that was expected to give them some knowledge of the country, but no contact with the enemy —there was a captain and four enlisted men.

One thing they had that Callaghen and the patrol's survivors did not have. They had water—plenty of water.

CHAPTER 2

Callaghen considered the odds and found no comfort in them. His men were obviously dehydrated, some in much worse shape than others. He knew the signs.

None of the men complained; they were beyond that. From their flushed skin, labored breathing, and sleepiness, he could judge their degree of exhaustion. Walsh was rubbing his arms and legs, and several times Callaghen had seen him shake his head. A tingling of the limbs, dizziness, and difficulty in breathing indicated that he was worse off than the wounded man. These symptoms would be followed by delirium, swollen tongue, and partial deafness.

If they could get water tomorrow . . . Walsh emptied his canteen, then made as if to throw it away.

"Don't do that, Walsh," Callaghen said. "If we get to water tomorrow, you'll need a canteen."

Walsh blinked, then shrugged, but he kept his canteen.

It was a long, slow day. The minutes seemed like hours, and the men mostly lay still, but once in a while one moved into a bit of shade, one man to a spot, for nowhere was there enough shade for two. Occasionally a shot splintered rock near them as the Mohaves let them know they were out there, waiting.

At sundown Callaghen got them up. Walsh he had to lift to his feet. Croker, rifle in the hollow of his arm, stood waiting. His features were drawn, but there was a cold determination in the man's face.

"Don't you fret about me, Irish," he said grimly. "When you get there, I'll be with you."

"I'm gambling on it."

They moved out, scattered a little, making a poor target in the dim light, and the Mohaves did not fire.

Callaghen looked at the mountain peak before them, and headed for it. As mountains went, it wasn't much, really, but it was their landmark, it was their hope. Once Walsh stumbled and fell, but he got up without help.

After an hour they halted. It was open country, nothing around them, and ahead it seemed to stretch even flatter and emptier.

When they went on, they saw the rocks drawing nearer again, the flat land becoming a shallow saucer with baked earth at the bottom where water must have stood after a sudden rain. There were a few scattered desert plants along the rim of this hollow, which afforded no real cover, but with these and the occasional brush they would at least be less of a target.

The Delaware staggered and almost fell, but braced himself with his rifle butt against the sand. He stood for a moment, swaying.

"How far would you guess?" Callaghen asked him.

"To the mountain? A mile, I think. A little farther to the water."

They rested then, and some of them slept. Callaghen did not. The Mohaves were out there, not far away, and they would know about the water, too. Would they guess that the soldiers knew? If so, they would try to stop them before they reached it.

Callaghen forced the dullness from his mind, forced himself to study the ground between themselves and the mountain ahead. From here on, every step they could take would be a victory; and safety, at least for the moment, lay where water was.

Eagle Mountain was ahead of them. Before them there was a long, shallow trough in the desert floor running toward the peak, a place where water must have run off, perhaps finding a way to the hollow where they had stopped.

When to turn to the right toward the water hole? He considered that, and was suddenly aware the sky was already gray. He roused the men and they started on.

For a hundred yards, two hundred yards, they walked

fairly well. Then Croker's legs began acting oddly. He stumbled, and could hardly keep from falling. Walsh did fall. The Delaware helped him up, almost lifting him to his feet, and holding him until he gained his balance.

Walking and stumbling, falling occasionally, the men made another two hundred yards. It was light enough to be able to make out tracks, but Callaghen saw none . . . and with water near there should have been tracks.

Suppose there was no water? Suppose that mountain ahead was not even Eagle Mountain? This was not the Delaware's native country, and he had been through here only once . . . he could be wrong. And if there was no water, they were dead men.

Walsh fell again. Again they helped him up. Callaghen looked at the mountain. By the look of it in the dim light, it was bare, basaltic rock. He glanced off to the right.

"All right." He had to try twice before he could get the words out. "We'll turn here."

Croker fell, trying to climb the fifteen-inch embankment. He struggled up, stared blankly at Callaghen, then steadied himself. "All right, Irish," he said. "I'm with you."

Walsh made it, and so did the Delaware. They were out in the open now; a shot struck into the dirt near them and they all knew this was a fight. They dropped to the ground.

"Hold your fire!" Callaghen spoke sharply. "Walsh, you and Croker can load. Try not to get any sand into the actions."

He waited. His own hands were not steady, his vision was blurred. He was further along toward dehydration than he had thought.

He rolled the dry pebble in his mouth. The skin on his hands looked wrinkled . . . like the hands of a very old man.

An Indian out there moved, and Callaghen fired without looking at his piece; he looked only at the Indian. The Mohave stumbled and fell.

That would put a scare into them. Indians were wise—they saw no advantage in a victory bought with the

death of their own warriors. They did not believe in losing men to gain ground, or losing a man for any reason
if it could be avoided. They were not afraid to die, but
they knew that a dead warrior kills no enemies.

"You got him." The Delaware shaped the words with
difficulty. "It is the first for us, I think."

Callaghen agreed. He had burned one other, he
thought, perhaps scratched him a bit. Nobody ever killed
as many Indians as he thought he had. When a report
came in of Indians killed in battle, he usually discounted
it by half.

The sun came up. In that shallow basin between the
ridges the heat was unbelievable. He waited, peering about
for enemies that never showed themselves. Walsh did not
move.

A slow, long hour went by, and then another. Callaghen
lay on the sand. He should move, he knew, for the heat
was more intense down here. He should move, but he
could not.

Yet he must. They must try for the water. "All right,"
he said aloud, and nobody stirred. "We will go now," he
said, but there was no movement, no response.

Summoning all his strength, he pushed himself up.
He got to his knees and slugged the Delaware. "Get up,
damn you!" he managed. *"Get up!"*

The Delaware got up, swaying on his feet. Then he
helped Croker to his feet, and between them they got
Walsh up.

Callaghen stood erect. The weight of the spare rifle,
slung across his back, was almost more than he could
stand. With his own rifle in hand, he peered around.

Only rocks and sand, sand and rocks. Sand, white and
pink and dirty gray, and above them the sullen rocks.
He turned squarely right. "March!" he said, and the
sound was choked and hoarse from his dry throat. He
tried to swallow, and found he could not. He stepped
out, almost fell, but then walked on.

Staggering, the others followed.

Suddenly a rider appeared, then another. The Mohaves
were closing in; they thought they had them now.

"Come on," Callaghen muttered. "Maybe not with a rifle, but with this pistol—"

The men behind him had stopped, but he turned, got behind them and drove them on, cursing hoarsely, waving his rifle.

Befuddled as he was, he could still see there were no tracks. Tracks meant water, they were fingers pointing the way to it; no tracks meant no water . . . But there *had* to be water.

He peered ahead, and saw that the Indians were not much over two hundred yards off now.

He plodded on, keeping the men together. Eagle Mountain was on his left now, and still no tracks. He fought back his dismay, and realized that his eyes were blurred.

Heat waves shimmered between himself and the Indians; even the mountain seemed unreal, lacking substance. Walsh was down again, and Callaghen stopped while the others got him up. He waited, his rifle up and threatening. Again they started on.

The Delaware turned toward him. "See? It is in the mesquite. Right ahead."

Past the point of rocks was a clump of mesquite, green and lovely. Certainly water could not be far. . . . The Mohaves were closer now.

"Be ready," Callaghen said. "After I fire, you fire, but give me a little time to reload." He looked at the others. "Can you fire?" he asked Croker.

"Try me," the wounded man replied grimly. Walsh stared at him dumbly, but he unslung his rifle. Well, he might not hit anything, but the act of firing itself would help.

They moved ahead and the Mohaves came closer. Deliberately Callaghen stopped, dropped to one knee on the blistering sand and held his rifle on the nearest Indian.

The man reined his horse around, dropped onto the far side of it, and rode on.

"Go ahead," he told the others. "Head for the mesquite."

He did not think the Indians knew about the pistol. He was saving that, hoping to draw them in close enough to get two or three before they could get away.

Only one of the Indians seemed to have a rifle. The others needed to get within bow shot, and he had heard somewhere that such weapons were not very effective unless within sixty yards. And at that distance, with a pistol, he knew what he could do.

They were brave men—brave, but not foolish. They wanted him dead, but most of all they wanted to be alive. They were wary of him, for he had shot one of them and killed him. He had wounded another, at least slightly. So he did not shoot now, but waited, letting them think about what he might do.

The soldiers ahead were beginning to hurry. He got up and walked on to join them. The water hole was supposed to be in that clump of mesquite, yet he had still seen no tracks. Nor were there bees, an almost certain indication of water if the bees were flying toward it.

He faced the situation calmly. He had been close to death too many times not to know that he was living on borrowed time. If there was water there they would drink, and if there was no water they would die. There was no chance of going farther, at least not for Walsh, and perhaps not for Croker.

He had been watching carefully, and he did not believe there were more than eight or ten Indians. They had water and they had horses and this was their country, over which they must have traveled before this, so the advantage was theirs. They had no need to return to a distant post; they had no need to report to a superior officer. The horses gave them mobility and they could ride far to water and ride back again, while the soldiers must move slowly, and with great care.

Some of the Mohaves were closing in again, but the soldiers kept moving. Suddenly one Indian dashed at Callaghen, but as he lifted his rifle the Indian wheeled and rode away. Behind him a yell sounded, and another Indian charged.

"Hold your fire!" Callaghen warned. "They want us to empty our guns so they can close in and wipe us out."

Deliberately he fell back to cover the retreat of the others. Croker was helping Walsh. The Delaware, rifle at the ready, was walking backwards, watching the Indians.

They came again in short, quick dashes, then wheeled to ride away. They raised up from their crude saddles and slapped their behinds derisively, taunting the white soldiers to get them to fire. Suddenly Indians on one side began to ride nearer. All eyes were on them. *All* eyes . . . !

Realizing that this was what the Indians wanted—for all eyes to be directed on them so the others could close in, Callaghen whirled. As he did so, they charged. He did not drop to one knee, but fired quickly, almost offhand.

His first shot caught a charging Indian full in the chest, knocking him backwards off his horse. At the same instant Callaghen dropped his rifle, drew his six-shooter, and fired, one, two, *three!*

An Indian pitched over with the first shot, a second wheeled his horse and took the bullet in the shoulder and side. The third was shot in the head.

From behind him he heard a shot, and another, and then the desert was empty, the Indians gone, except one who lay sprawled and dead on the desert.

Holstering the pistol, Callaghen followed after the others, loading his rifle as he walked.

Croker stared at him. "Man, that was shootin'! I never seen the like!"

They broke through the mesquite, and saw a bare patch of sand, a basin of cracked mud, and no water.

No water . . .

CHAPTER 3

Despair gripped Callaghen for a moment. "Croker," he said, "get back there with your rifle. The Mohaves knew about this, and they may hang back for a time, but they'll be coming on."

"I do not think so," the Delaware said. "I think it has cost them too much, and they will not risk your shooting again."

Callaghen sat down and carefully reloaded his pistol. As he did so he considered the situation. This basin was at the lowest point around. It lay at the end of a ridge of rocks where a spring might conceivably be, surrounded by mesquite and a healthy growth of salt grass. The place was a natural catch basin for water draining off the rocky ridges around it.

"The mesquite is an indicator of ground water. So is salt grass." Callaghen spoke slowly, for his tongue felt swollen and clumsy, and his lips were cracked.

The Delaware looked at him with dull eyes. Walsh sprawled on the sand, making no sound. He lay in shade under the mesquite growth which towered six to seven feet above him.

Callaghen's own head seemed not to be working too well, but he tried to focus his attention on recalling what he knew about this plant. While it was regarded as a sure indicator of water, the roots might penetrate fifty feet into the earth. On the other hand, the roots of salt grass rarely went beyond ten feet, and the water table where the salt grass grew was often less than three feet beneath the surface.

He put down his rifle, unslung the spare he had carried, and went into the basin. Throwing aside the slabs of cracked mud, he began to dig. The earth at the bottom was sand and clay, and it was very dry—dry as a buffalo skull that has lain twenty years out on the prairie.

On his knees, he worked with his hands, digging. He did not think about the parched earth. He did not think about the sting of the alkali when it got into cuts on his hands; he thought only of the water below.

Croker came back, staring dully at him, intent on his digging. "You waste your time. We are dead men," he said.

Callaghen did not look up. "Get back to your duty," he said hoarsely. "Watch for the Mohaves."

"They are gone."

"Go back and watch for them!"

Croker did not move. "You are not an officer. You have no authority here."

Callaghen stood up stiffly and turned around. "Croker, you've got one chance to live. You get back to your job, or I'll kill you."

Croker hesitated, but then he turned and went back through the mesquite, and Callaghen dropped to his knees again.

He was a tall man, with wide shoulders, a well-setup man who ordinarily moved easily and with some grace. Around the post he was something of a mystery. Everyone knew that his enlistment period would soon be over. When he enlisted he had given his home as Boston. He had twice been advanced to sergeant and had twice been broken back to private, each time for fighting. He was known among those who served with him as a rough fighter, a good man to leave alone.

He drank rarely and sparingly, read a great deal, and had few real friends, although he was friendly enough. He rarely spoke of himself. He was proficient with all weapons, and was a superb horseman.

Croker, who had served with him for more than a year, had never known him to receive mail. He was really a loner. Many a man who joined the Indian-fighting army did so because he wished to disappear . . . and the rate of desertion was high.

Now he continued to dig steadily. A foot . . . two feet. The hole was still dry, and he was gasping for breath. The heat, the lack of water, and the long exhausting march had taken their toll, but he went on digging. Finally the Delaware came and pushed him aside, and after that they took turns.

Callaghen was down four feet before he felt dampness in the earth. He grunted suddenly and began digging harder. The sand grew damper, and finally it began actually to ooze water. The Delaware pressed his face against the sand thrown up at the edge, feeling its coolness.

Callaghen went on digging. The work was harder now, for the sand was firmly packed, but he gouged out great handfuls and tossed them on the growing bank. At last he sat back, hands hanging, and watched. Slowly, water began to seep into the hole.

He dipped up a little, and touched his lips with it, letting a few drops fall on his tongue. A drop or two went down his throat, and he felt a delicious coolness go all through him.

When he could get a few mouthfuls down his throat, he took up his rifle and walked out to where Croker sat. "Go on back for a while," he said. "There's water there."

Croker stared at him, incredulous. Then he scrambled to his feet, and fell. He got up slowly, and went back through the mesquite.

Callaghen sat down and let his eyes sweep the terrain before him. Their position was not a bad one, the only real danger lying in the rocks behind them. But he detected no movement there.

They were going to make it back. Of that he could feel sure now. None of them was in shape for a long march, but with water they could make it; once they filled their canteens he doubted the Mohaves would follow them . . . unless their numbers were greatly increased.

He began to think out a route, estimating the distances they must make, and the time it would take. It was time that they must think of. With luck they could find more water on the way, but they would have long marches, and no food.

The Mohaves really seemed to have gone. He studied

the land ahead of them. There was a spring in the Ibex Mountains to the southeast, he knew. Trying to recall what he had learned from listening to Indians, to travelers, trappers, and occasional prospectors, he decided the spring must be twelve to fifteen miles away, a difficult walk for men in their condition, but now that they had water it was possible.

After a while he went back to the water hole. It was half filled with muddy water now, and he drank sparingly. Croker was lying on his face, his head on his arm, asleep. The Delaware was sitting back, his head tilted against a rock. Walsh was sleeping.

"You brought us through," the Indian said quietly. "You are a good man, Callaghen. I think you have been an officer before this."

"We have a long way to go," was Callaghen's reply. He squatted on his heels where he could watch the approach from under the brush. "Do you know Ibex Spring?" he asked.

"I have heard of it. I have not been there."

"Can you do twelve miles?"

"Yes, I think so. With water, we can go as far as you wish." He brought his head into position. "You are a good man with a gun, Callaghen, and you are a good leader. You knew about mesquite and salt grass as indicators of water. What else do you know?"

"That I am tired, and it is your turn to go on watch."

The Delaware got up and stretched. The water in the hole was clearing as the silt settled to the bottom, and he drank long and deep, then drank once again.

When he got up, he wiped his mouth with the back of his hand. "I think the lieutenant should have talked to you," he said.

"What does that mean?"

"Did you not know that he questioned everybody about the desert? He was a very young man, and he wanted to know a great deal."

"He was a shrewd young man, then. That's one way of learning." Callaghen paused. "When one is to travel in a new area, one had better learn all he can."

The Delaware smiled. "I suppose so, but that did not account for all of his questions."

The Indian left him, and after Callaghen drank again he lay down on the sand. Night would soon be here. He thought of his feet. He should bathe them, but he was afraid if he took his boots off he would never get them on again, for his feet would swell. They were blistered, he knew, and it must be the same with the feet of all the others.

What had the Delaware meant about the questions the lieutenant had asked, he wondered. It was natural for a man who was new to a country to ask questions.

They moved out into the desert when the stars were out, and a cool wind blew low across the earth. Scarcely a leaf stirred, the wind was soft and easy, and the only sound was the whisper of their footsteps in the sand. Their canteens were full.

The night was long before them. Callaghen set an easy pace, moving along as if his feet did not hurt and as if he had only a few miles to go. When they had walked an hour, they stopped for ten minutes.

The Delaware walked out into the desert to sit down, and when they started again he joined them and said, "I do not think we are followed, but that means nothing."

The mountains were on their right, raw, hard-edged mountains of rock thrust up from the desert floor, neither friendly or unfriendly, only indifferent.

Callaghen had traveled many walking miles, or miles on horse or camel, and he could judge distance fairly well. In the first hour they made about two and a half miles. They would do as well in the second. In the third it would be perhaps two miles, for the men would be getting tired and there was a narrow ridge to cross.

The lieutenant had taken them farther north than Callaghen had at first believed—too far north. As he walked Callaghen began for the first time to think about that young lieutenant, suddenly puzzled by incongruities.

It was the Delaware's comment that had started his curiosity, but now he found more and more to puzzle about. So many things had indicated the lieutenant was new to the West and to the desert, and yet he had obviously guided their march by certain landmarks. These might have been given him by their commanding officer except that he, too, was new to this country.

Callaghen did not know the orders for the patrol. Only the lieutenant and the C.O. had known their mission. All the men had been told was that they were to familiarize themselves with the country, and to see if any Mohaves were in the area.

They had done that. They had scouted north, farther north than seemed necessary when one considered that the desert troops were to protect freighters and stages along the Government Road. But they had located the Indians ... or had been located by them.

Now the lieutenant was dead, so one would never know exactly what he was trying to determine.

Thoughtfully, Callaghen went over in his mind the questions the lieutenant had asked, and what implications there were in what he had said. The one comment that stuck in Callaghen's mind was one about horse thieves needing water and grazing for their stock, and the difficulty of finding it.

On their march north they had skirted the Owl's Head Mountains, and had stopped briefly at the springs called the Owl Holes. The water there was not very good, but on the lieutenant's orders the catch basin was cleaned out and left in fine shape.

At daylight they reached Ibex Spring, drank deep, refilled their canteens, and found shade in which to rest. The day dragged on, but before nightfall they started south, keeping the mountains on their right. When they had been walking a little more than an hour a faint trail appeared, and they left the one they had followed and crossed over a low saddle and marched down the western side of the mountains.

It was a short march, but Callaghen knew the men's condition and insisted on stopping. At the springs at the southern tip of the range they camped until night came. Then they marched south once more, again only a short march—no more than ten miles to Cave Springs. But the march was uphill, and much of it was on soft sand.

At Cave Springs they bathed their feet, rested, and thought of food.

"How far to where we can get help?" Croker wanted to know. "I've had enough of this."

"You've got a tough pull ahead of you," Callaghen answered. "It's twenty miles to Bitter Springs, and that's our first chance. We might find somebody stopping there. And then there's a long trek back to Camp Cady."

Croker swore, and Walsh stared at Callaghen, then looked down at his boots. "I got a notion to stay right here," he said. "I don't think I can make it."

"You'll make it," Callaghen said cheerfully. "No use to waste all the steps you've taken."

Walsh looked thoughtful as he saw the way Croker's eyes remained on Callaghen. Walsh was keenly sensitive to the strengths and weaknesses of other men. A coward himself, he had no envy for the brave, although in his own way he respected them, and he feared them as willing to do things he might hesitate to do.

There was something in Croker's eyes now that puzzled him, some peculiar intentness that set him to wondering. Croker had no reason for hating Callaghen, and Walsh was quite sure he did not, but had someone less perceptive seen that look they might have suspected that he did. And there was something else. That look of Croker's had been an estimating, measuring glance . . . and there was greed in it.

Walsh could think of no reason why that should be so, but he sensed suddenly that Callaghen might be standing between Croker and something he wanted.

Shortly before midnight on the third day after that the four men walked into Camp Cady.

The shelters were miserable hovels built of logs and brush, but there was water there, and there was food, and there was rest.

"Private Callaghen?" The voice of the soldier who spoke was brisk. "The captain would like to see you at once." He turned and pointed. "Right over there. At the end of the line."

CHAPTER 4

Captain Hill was seated on a camp chair in his under-
shirt, suspenders hanging, when Callaghen entered. He
was unshaven and he looked tired.

"You wished to see me, sir?"

"What happened out there?" Captain Hill asked.

Callaghen's report was brief and concise. Hill listened,
rubbing his jaw thoughtfully. Then he got to his feet and
swore softly.

He took a map from a group of several that leaned
against the side of his bed. He spread the map open on
the table. "Can you show me, Callaghen, just where you
were when attacked?"

"Yes, sir." Callaghen put his finger on the spot and
stepped back.

"What in God's name was Allison doing away up
there? Did he say anything to you about it, Callaghen?
Did he give you any idea why?"

"No, sir. I understood we were merely to learn the
lay of the land and try to judge by surface indications
what movement there had been . . . by tracks, sir."

Hill sat down abruptly. "Callaghen, how long have you
been in the service?"

"Three years, sir."

"Your time is just about up, then?"

"Yes, sir. I have ten days to go, sir."

"You have been a sergeant twice, I believe. What
caused them to break you?"

"Fighting, sir."

"*Fighting?* Damn it, what are they thinking of? I'd
sooner break a man for not fighting. All right, Callaghen,

22

I need some help. As of now you are a sergeant again."

He looked up suddenly, sharply. "You are an educated man, Callaghen. Were you ever an officer?"

Callaghen hesitated the briefest moment. "Yes, sir. Several times."

"Broken for fighting, I suppose?" Hill suggested sarcastically.

"No, sir. I moved on." Again he paused briefly. "I am Irish, sir. In these days that practically means I am a man without a country. Those of us with military training fight wherever there is employment."

"Did you serve with Meagher?"

"Yes, sir."

"All right, all right. You say you have Allison's things. Go to his quarters, Callaghen, and put his things together. He was not with me long enough to get acquainted, but he had a family, I believe."

Callaghen waited a moment. "After I sleep, sir?"

"Oh, of course! I'm sorry, Callaghen. You've had a rough go of it. I will want to get a complete report later. Having been an officer, I suppose you know how to write a report. Please do so. I shall want to know all I can about the Mohaves, the water, the terrain . . . you understand."

It was noon before Callaghen got up. His feet were blistered, and he treated them as best he could. All was quiet. Only eight men were in camp, aside from Captain Hill, and at least three of the others were, as he was, in no shape for duty after the long march.

He dressed and shaved, and then went to Lieutenant Allison's quarters.

He stepped into the crudely constructed shelter and stopped, startled by what he saw. Somebody had been there before him, for Allison's duffel bag had been opened and the contents dumped on his cot. His things had been hurriedly searched, letters ripped open—everything had been gone through.

He stepped to the door, and lifted the flap of canvas that did duty for a door. He studied the ground outside carefully, but there were too many footprints to determine anything. Any one of the men might have come here, searching for money or whatever else they could find of value.

He went next door to the captain's quarters, where he reported to Captain Hill. Hill went back with him and stared around Allison's quarters.

"Thieves! As if we didn't have trouble enough out here without having blasted thieves among us! Eight men, and how do we know which one it was?"

"Seven men, sir. I came here on the captain's orders, and I would have had no reason for this."

Carefully, Callaghen gathered together the things that had belonged to the lieutenant. Allison had been a neat, meticulous sort of man. His uniforms were new, showing no wear. *All* his clothes were new. This was an unusual thing for a man who has seen much duty.

Puzzled, Callaghen examined them again. At least one uniform, he was sure, had never been worn. At least one pair of boots had not been worn. The cavalry saber, bright and shining, that hung from a nail in the corner could also have been new.

One by one he checked and listed the articles, and when he had finished, he sat down on the bed. Everything Lieutenant Allison had possessed was new; and whatever else he had planned, he had not planned to stay. He had none of those things an officer brings to a new, desert station, those little things that can make one's camp life more pleasant. No pictures, no papers, no books. Not even extra soap . . . nothing. And he had yet to look at the things Allison had carried on his person.

These he now put down on the table before him. There were a ring with three keys, a few odd coins, and in a small leather poke, ten gold eagles—a good sum for an army officer to be carrying. There was also a letter, and a receipt for storage of a trunk, which had been left at a hotel in Los Angeles. And last of all, put inside the poke in such a way that it seemed merely another thickness . . . a rectangular piece of doeskin, and on it some arrows, circles, and rows of xx's.

It was a map of the Mohave Desert, the xx's indicating mountain ranges; the circles were waterholes. Death Valley was not shown; the Colorado River, however, was drawn with great care. The west coast and the mountains separating the desert from the sea were not shown. To one who did not know the desert, the map would mean little, and there was no indication of what it might be meant to show.

Whoever had drawn it had no exact knowledge of the desert. Several small mountain ranges were left out, by accident or on purpose. The only section drawn with any detail, was of a rugged range of mountains that lay to the east of where they had ridden on patrol, and of the route that led to it from the Colorado River.

After a moment's thought, Callaghen put the map inside his shirt, and carefully packed everything else, and carried the duffel bag and saber to Captain Hill's quarters.

Hill glanced at the things. "You take charge of them. There will be a rider leaving for San Bernardino tomorrow. Send it with him."

Callaghen walked back to his shelter. Croker looked up as he entered. He looked at the duffel bag. "You fixin' up Allison's gear? Too bad about him."

"He was a good man. I think he would have made it."

"You got to learn fast out here. When it comes to Injuns, if you flunk the course you lose your hair."

Croker studied the duffel bag. "He didn't carry much, did he? You'd figure a man of family, like he was, would carry more stuff to make things easy. Last post I was on, when a young officer came in he brought all sorts of extra grub, and other things."

"I know nothing about Allison's family. He did leave an address—a sister, or something. I am sending his stuff to her."

"Yeah? Hill sure depends on you. What you got on him?"

"Nothing," Callaghen said. "He needs help, that's all. With Allison gone, he has no one to help."

He did not like Croker, and wanted to avoid his questions, but did not want to make an issue of it. The man was tough. He had a bad flesh wound, but once it was bound up he had come through the long march in better shape than Walsh, who was unhurt. Good or bad, the man was a stayer, and he was the kind the frontier needed.

Callaghen's mind was busy with the curious map. He thought that whoever had gone through Allison's stuff had been looking for it . . . but it might have been somebody just hoping to find a bottle of whiskey.

The map now . . . it was obviously old. Whoever had made it had worked from the Colorado River westward and northward, and apparently knew nothing at all of the country that lay between this camp and the coast.

Nor did the mountain ranges lie as they should. The mapmaker had probably had no compass, and had not been able to locate himself in relation to the cardinal points. The skin was beautifully tanned, probably by an Indian.

But why a map at all? And how had Allison come into possession of it?

He considered Captain Hill. A good man, but a tired one. Nearing fifty years of age, without influence and probably without anything spectacular in his record, he would be shunted from post to post now, with no hope of promotion. A good man lost in the shuffle. He would be nearing retirement, a patient man who did his duty from day to day, just one of the men who help to make the whole machine work.

As he cleaned his rifle and the pistol he had acquired from the lieutenant, Callaghen considered all the aspects of the situation. Gradually, he got his gear in shape, and with the Delaware, he led the horses to fresh pasture, where the Indian remained on guard.

Starting back, he saw something move in the brush ahead. He walked on, but as he passed that particular clump of brush he glanced down. Boot tracks in the earth . . . it was Croker, then. He had seen those tracks often enough on their long march. Croker was watching him . . . why?

Croker must suspect that he had found something in the lieutenant's equipment, and Croker was a greedy man. Did he know more than he himself did? Or was the man just hoping for anything of value?

Come to think of it, Croker had arrived in camp in

Allison's company, together with that easterner and the kid from Minnesota.

It was hot and still outside. Off across the sandy plain a dust devil danced briefly, then lost itself somewhere among the greasewood. It was a miserable, God-forsaken place in which to serve one's time, and yet—he squinted his eyes against the glare and looked at the far-off hills, lost in the blue—it was a good country . . . for those who did not fight it.

That was the secret of the desert. One had to accommodate one's self to it. To the vast loneliness, the distances, the far-off hazy mountains, to the shadows they took on at dawn or at sunset. There was harshness in this land, but there was beauty too. It was a country a man could grow to love.

He fought the Indians out here because they fought him, but in a way he understood them, too. At least, he believed he did.

His time here was short—only a few days longer. He had forgotten to sew on his stripes, forgotten to mention them. Well, no matter. In a few days he would be free of the army, and he could go wherever he wished.

But *where?* Back to Ireland? Back to Boston? What was there for him in either place? Boston was just a city where he had stopped for a time . . . and there had been so many other cities, other places. He was used to the army way, and it had been a long time since there had been any other, except for short periods.

Like so many others, he had been running when he joined the army, escaping from the past, trying to lose himself in its routine.

His career had been little different from that of many another Irish soldier of fortune. His name had been O'Callaghan in Ireland, an ancient and honored name, but after the ill-fated rebellion of 1848 he had fled the country, by the first ship he could get on, which was one to Canada.

The gold rush was on, and he crossed Canada and went down the west coast to California, where he panned gold on the Trinity, and from the first pan had found color. Finally he went to San Francisco, where he was shanghaied, and when he again realized where he was he found himself at sea, his gold gone.

He jumped ship in North Africa, and being without money and in danger of arrest, he joined the French army. For two years he campaigned in the Sahara, was wounded and discharged; and after recuperating he found his way to Afghanistan and joined the army there, entering the service as an officer of artillery. He advanced rapidly, but after the capture of Kandahar he left this service, spent some time in India, and at last reached Shanghai, where he served in Francis Townsend Ward's army in 1862 and 1863. It was after the capture of Soochow that he left.

Once again in the United States, he had joined the Irish Brigade and fought at Chancellorsville, The Wilderness, Spotsylvania Court House, and Cold Harbor.

Now, at thirty-four, with only a few days left of his army service, Callaghen had three hundred dollars saved, and a plan to go to that California that lay beyond the mountains, a decision of only the last few days.

Captain Hill emerged from his quarters into the glare of the sun. "Callaghen? You had better sew on your stripes. You have some, I suppose?"

Callaghen smiled. "I saved them, sir. I figured they might come in handy."

"You were with the Irish Brigade, I believe? You'll be getting out just in time, I think. There's going to be a new commanding officer here."

"Sir?"

"It will be Major Ephraim Sykes, and he doesn't like the Irish."

Callaghen felt the icy touch of premonition. "I know the major, sir. And I know what he thinks of the Irish. And of me."

CHAPTER 5

The captain was surprised. "You know the Major?" he asked.

"Yes, sir. We met briefly on several occasions. He's one of those who believe we Irish are second-class citizens. I understand that before the war he operated a business where he had a sign: NO IRISH NEED APPLY."

"I have heard something to that effect. Well, we will hope that your papers come through before he arrives."

"We Irish are used to it, Captain Hill. We had it in Ireland for years, from the British. The Catholic Irish were allowed no schools of their own. For many years no Irish craftsman was allowed an apprentice. Priests had to go into hiding, or leave the country entirely. It was very rough."

"And you?"

"I left, sir. I came over here for a while—tried prospecting in California."

Hill glanced at him quickly. *"You* did? You know something about minerals, then?"

"A little. Most of that I learned in Asia, later."

"You should spend some time in the desert. There are all sorts of rumors, Callaghen. Some say there are vast deposits of gold and silver right here in the Mohave."

His voice lowered a little. "Have you heard of the River of Gold? They say it runs through a cave under the desert."

Callaghen shrugged. "There are always those stories, sir. You know when the Moslems conquered all of North Africa in the eighth century the Christians disappeared. Of course, most of them were converted to Mohammedan-

29

ism very suddenly. It was the only thing to do if one wanted to survive. But some were killed, and some left the country . . . in any event, they vanished.

"As a result, there are strange stories that come out of the Sahara. Mysterious sounds are heard in the desert at night. The Berbers and the Tuaregs say the sounds come from cities under the ground, and in those cities the Christians are hiding until the right time comes for them to return."

Captain Hill chuckled. "They'll wait a long time, I'm thinking. Nonetheless, Callaghen, if I were a younger man and getting out of the army, I might give a little thought to the matter. You know, some of these desert rivers have gone underground, so why couldn't it be that they had hollowed out caves there? And if there were gold in the rock . . .?"

Several days passed in routine duty. On more than one occasion Captain Hill detailed three-man patrols to scout the country around, and each time they saw Indians. Twice they were fired on and returned the fire, but with no visible results on either side. Every day they scanned the road, hoping for the promised relief. The horses and mules were taken each morning to the sparse pasture, and guarded carefully. Several times Mohaves were seen in the proximity of the camp.

Twice trains of freight wagons went through, bound for the Colorado. The freighters were tough men, desert-seasoned and well-armed, yet on each occasion they lost horses to the Indians, and once a man was wounded. A prospector was killed within a few miles of La Paz.

Adobe buildings had at one time been built on the present campsite, but as the army had maintained no permanent station there, they had been allowed to fall into ruin. Sudden floods had damaged some of them; in others the hastily made roofs were in need of repair. During the hottest weather the men preferred the brush shelters where a breeze could blow through.

Callaghen led the repair work on several of the buildings, especially on some that were close together, always being careful to leave a good field of fire in case of defense by a small group. For months the army had been promising a good-sized detachment, but it had not come. And neither had Callaghen's discharge papers arrived.

One day when Captain Hill came to inspect some of the construction, Callaghen said to him, "Sir, about Lieutenant Allison—may I ask if you were notified of his coming?"

"What kind of a question is that?"

"It's simply that I suspect, sir, that he was not a proper officer. He had *been* an officer; he knew the routine. But I think that he was not actually in the service now, but came here for reasons of his own."

"Why would he want to do that?"

"Why not? If he knew what would be required of him, he would then be able to explore the desert for days or even weeks with a military escort. Communication is not good out here, sir, as you know. It is often thirty to sixty days between communications from headquarters. Knowing that, an officer could arrive, cover a good bit of country, and then disappear before anyone knew any better."

"But why? No man in his right mind is going to ask for duty in this desert."

"That's just it, sir. He might have been looking for something. You yourself mentioned a river of gold. You suggested prospecting."

Hill waved a hand carelessly. "That was just talk. Of course, any such place as this is bound to produce stories, legends—but they're nonsense, Callaghen, utter nonsense. This desert is a corner of hell—several thousand square miles of sand, rocky ridges, and cacti, with no water at all, or bad water. A desert is a place unfit for man, and that's why they call it a desert."

Mercer was guarding the stock when Callaghen joined him. It was a clear, lovely desert morning, not yet hot. The morning sun left shadows in the canyons, but caused the ridges to reveal themselves with a stark clarity. One really never knew mountains unless he had seen them at both sunrise and sunset.

"Beautiful country here, Mercer. . . . Aren't you from Minnesota?"

"That's right. It's all very different there. The Indians

are different, too. We have the Sioux, and some Chippewas."

"You joined the unit with Lieutenant Allison, didn't you?"

"Yes. That is, we had our orders and were waiting for the stage. He came up and joined us, and said he was going to Cady."

"Too bad to have lost him. I think he'd have made a good officer." He paused just a moment. "I forwarded his things to his sister. I don't believe he had any other relatives."

"He had some friends in Los Angeles, Sergeant. One, at least. He was talking to a man at the Bella Union before he spoke to us—a very sharp-looking man with a broken nose."

"Chance acquaintance, probably."

"I don't think so. At least, he trusted him enough to let him hold his orders for him. I saw the man give him his orders at the stage. It was the same envelope Lieutenant Allison turned over to Captain Hill."

Holding orders, or delivering them? Callaghen watched the horses, talking idly with Mercer on half a dozen topics. Then he went back to the compound and stepped suddenly into his quarters. Croker was there, and he had Callaghen's duffel bag upon a cot, open.

"What the hell goes on here?"

Croker turned sharply. "I was out of smokin'. Thought you might have some."

"I don't smoke. I never have."

Croker's smile was forced. "Say, that's right! Now, why didn't I recall that?"

"Stay out of my gear, Croker. I won't tell you again."

"Sure, Sarge. I'll stay out, but don't you get too pushy. Sergeant or no, I'll take some of that out of you."

"Anytime."

Croker pushed by him and went out. There had been nothing in the bag for anyone to look at, nothing except the usual things a soldiering man might have.

But Croker was suspicious. Of what? Or was he, like Callaghen himself, merely guessing at something? He might know something, or he might simply be of a suspicious mind.

Callaghen shaded his eyes and looked over the desert. The Indians were out there now, you could be sure of that. Captain Hill and only eight men here, with never enough ammunition or food on hand . . . if the Mohaves only realized it they could sweep over this station at any time.

After bringing the horses into the corrals, Callaghen posted guards. Captain Hill seemed willing to leave matters in his hands, and he was prepared to assume whatever responsibility was given him.

Night came suddenly, as do all desert nights. One moment the sun's rays were turning the mountain ridges scarlet and gold . . . and then the sun was gone and the stars were there.

Croker and Beamis had the first guard. Beamis was a raw recruit just out from Pennsylvania. Whatever else Croker was, he was a frontiersman and a soldier. He knew what slackness meant, and he would stand for none of it. Beamis wanted only one thing—to get out of the army.

"Can't you speak to the captain, Sergeant?" he said to Callaghen. "I have no business here. I just got mad at my wife and enlisted to show her. Now I'm not mad at her any more."

Callaghen had to smile. "Doesn't pay to move too quick, Beamis. I'm sorry, but you're in and you'll have to stay."

"You mean I can't get out? What kind of a deal is that?"

"You joined, and now you'll have to fill out your time. There's no two ways about it."

"But what about my wife? She'll leave me!"

"If she does, you're better off without her. Settle down, man. You bought your ticket, now take your ride."

He walked back to the encampment. The moon was rising, and there was already a thin glow over the mountain. It would be a tricky night, for on such a moonlit night shadows appear to move, and one may suddenly develop a feeling that a shadow is an Indian.

It was very still. Captain Hill came outside his quarters. "It's been a good life, Callaghen," he said, "and I shall miss it."

"You've been a soldier all your life, sir?"

"Not quite. Before the war I quit for four years. If I'd stayed in I might be a general now. A colonel, at least. But the peacetime army wasn't much, and I'd had enough duty at the forts on the plains. I quit and opened a store."

"Like General Grant."

"Yes, but I was successful. I did quite well, in fact, and then the guerillas burned me out and I lost everything. So I went back into the army. If I'd gone in a year sooner I'd have made it."

"There are always ifs, sir."

Hill turned his head to look at Callaghen. "You say you've met Sykes before this?"

"Yes, sir. It was he who broke me from sergeant . . . both times."

"Want to tell me about it?"

"Well, you know how some people think about the Irish. We're despised in a lot of places, and there are even hotels where we aren't accepted, restaurants where we are refused service. Sykes was worse than most.

"I knew nothing of that, but he was having trouble with his Chinese laundryman. He was berating the man frightfully, and seemed about to strike him. I offered my services."

"You what?"

"I offered to interpret, sir. I speak Chinese."

Hill stared at him. *"Chinese?* You do?"

"I speak seven languages, sir, and half a dozen dialects. Well, sir, he told me what to tell the man and I did, and managed to straighten the matter out. I saluted, and was about to leave when he called me back and told me never, under any circumstances, to interfere again."

"And then?"

"He was on me, sir. He found out I was Irish, although he should have guessed it before. I got all the rough duty. But it was the girl who really made the difference."

"A girl?"

"Yes, sir. She came to the post to visit someone she had known as a child, and I was detailed to ride escort when she went riding.

"She kept looking at me, sir, and suddenly she said she had seen me before. She asked me again what my name was, and when I told her she recognized it. She had known me before, Captain . . . outside of Soochow, in China. I'd come up to an old temple with a small command. I was a major, sir, in Ward's outfit—Gordon's outfit by that time. The Ever-Victorious Army, they called it. She was just a skinny kid then, and she'd been stopped near the temple. She, her mother, and a doctor had run there for shelter from some of the rebels. We fought our way out of there and took them with us."

"And you were a major then? You've had quite a career, Callaghen."

He shrugged. "Ward had picked up his army off the waterfronts, Captain. He had scum of the earth, and right alongside them some of the finest fighting men in the world. He enlisted men of all nationalities, and he didn't screen them. Combat did that for him, and we were in battle almost constantly. Seventy per cent of the men had served in other armies—there were a couple of hundred Irishmen in the outfit. When Chinese Gordon took command he had a trained battle outfit. A man couldn't go wrong with them."

"Did Sykes know about the girl's recognizing you?"

"He saw us talking, and he was furious. I was an enlisted man and I was being too friendly. Of course, Malinda spoke up, and in the midst of it her father appeared. He'd always been grateful to me for getting his family out of that situation, so we had a long talk, and Sykes just faded out.

"Two days later I was transferred. They were building a new outfit for frontier service, and I found myself one of the cadre that would form it."

"And that left him with the girl?"

"No, sir. Malinda had a mind of her own, and she was suspicious about the transfer. No, sir. I am afraid it didn't do him much good."

CHAPTER 6

Major Ephraim Sykes was a man of definite mind. Positive in his opinions, he approached every problem knowing that there could be just two possibilities: his way and the wrong way. The opinions he held had been absorbed with his mother's milk, and nothing subsequent to that time had served to alter even one of them.

He was tall, handsome, immaculate in appearance. He was gracious, polite, and considerate to those he regarded as existing on his level. Others he ignored, or considered only with contempt. An only child, he had been brought up to believe that as an Anglo-Saxon white man of the right church, the right schools, and the right social position, any decision he made was of course the correct one.

He had been born on the right street in a medium-size town where his father operated the largest of the town's three banks. In school he had been bright but without brilliance, capable but without imagination, and he had graduated close to the top of his class. At the beginning of the War Between the States he had been given a commission, and he had advanced rapidly to the rank of major, partly by virtue of a cavalry charge in which he smashed the enemy at a crucial moment, driving them from their position and so turning the tide of battle.

A fact that he had conveniently forgotten was that the charge had begun when his horse ran away with him, and his men followed. Uncomfortable about the praise that came his way, he had gradually forgotten how the charge had begun, and modestly said it was nothing. He

36

had, he said, been fortunate enough to detect a weakness in the enemy line at that point.

The war ended too soon for him, for he had hoped to become a general—or at least a colonel. Failing that, despite the surplus of officers after the war, he had hoped to be sent to a good station where he might win a smashing victory over the Indians—the Plains Indians, of course, who had dash and glamour as fighting men.

The immigrant Irish were despised by many of the "right" people, so he despised them. The only Irish with whom he had ever had contact were a group who had settled on the edge of his town to build a spur of track for the railroad. Many of them drank too much, and most of them seemed to be amused by him, and this offended his dignity. In the army he had a few Irishmen in his command, and they, too, drank too much and were amused by him.

As his father's partner, he owned a part of a small shoe-manufacturing plant, as well as the bank. At the plant they hired no Irish, but that attitude was quite frequent at the time, and aroused no comment.

He had found no girl who appealed to him for more than the moment until he met Malinda Colton. Her family was of the best. Her father was a diplomat, her uncle a general. On two or three occasions he had escorted her to dinner or to other affairs, and when he found her talking on intimate terms with Callaghen—at least, both of them were laughing and seemed very friendly— he had been coldly furious.

The fact that Callaghen had once had rank equal to his own did not impress him. "Miss Colton," he told her gently, "the man is a vagabond, a soldier of fortune. He's—he's *Irish!*"

That Malinda did not take him seriously was irritating. She had said then, "So was General Thomas Francis Meagher, of the Irish Brigade. He married a very good friend of ours, and they have been blissfully happy."

Sykes was wise enough to drop the subject. Besides, he was on shaky ground, for it suddenly occurred to him that his commanding officer at the time was General Sheridan, who was the son of an Irish immigrant.

Now he found himself leading three troops of cavalry to occupy several forts in the Mohave Desert, in Indian country. The Indians were not the Sioux or the Cheyennes, but he had no doubt that he could win a victory over them.

There was one other thing. He had in his keeping the discharge papers for one Private Morty Callaghen, a name he had cause to remember. Twice, on flimsy excuses, he had broken Callaghen from sergeant to private, once by his order, once by his influence. And there is perhaps no one hated more by a man than one to whom he has done an injustice.

It was to the dispute over Callaghen that he laid his failure with Malinda Colton. And now he was to meet the man again. It was just his luck that Callaghen was about to be discharged.

The thought came to him that if the discharge was not delivered it would not be in effect. It was a fine point. Was Callaghen discharged when his papers were issued, or when they were delivered to him?

He dismissed the idea and his thoughts turned to his command. He was to garrison forts at Marl Springs, Bitter Springs, Rock Springs, and Fort Piute, as his judgment saw fit, to insure the safe passage of freight caravans and stages along the Government Road. He was to make no move against the Mohaves unless they first attacked him. His mission was to protect the road.

Major Sykes had never before seen the desert. He had come to California by ship. He had no idea what the "forts" were that he was to garrison, nor what a campaign in the desert could be like. He had heard of desert fighting, he had talked with officers who had fought the Apaches in New Mexico and Texas. He was quite sure he could handle the situation, his only doubt being what he might be able to make of it.

Camp Cady was on the Mohave River. He envisioned an imposing post beside a sparkling stream. There would be boating perhaps.

His first sight of the desert from the top of the pass was a shock. Captain Marriott, the second in command, commented, "There's a lot of desert out there. Fourteen thousand square miles, they say, depending on whose figures you use."

"That's impossible, Captain! That's larger than the state of Massachusetts."

"Yes, sir. And you can add part of Connecticut for good measure. That's a lot of rugged country, sir, and there's very little water."

Major Sykes was appalled. Never in his wildest speculations had he considered such a vast expanse of desert, and it was his job to patrol the Government Road through that wasteland with just three troops of soldiers!

"Have you served in the desert, Marriott?"

"No, sir, but I've traveled through it. Water is the problem. Water enough for a troop of men is hard to find."

"How do the Indians manage?"

"They scatter, sir. They know tiny water holes or seeps with just enough for one or two men. By the time they and their horses drink it may take hours to fill up again."

It was sundown when they rode into Camp Cady, and Sykes's spirits hit rock bottom. There were trees offering some shade, and there was the river—a mere trickle, by his standards. The huts were built of adobe or logs, and roofed with brush. Some of the soldiers actually lived in brush huts, preferring them in warm weather.

Captain Hill awaited him. "You'll be tired, sir. I've had water heated, so if you'd like a bath—"

"You haven't formed the men?"

"There are only eight men, sir. Three are on guard duty at present, and the others have just returned from a patrol."

The casualness of it offended him, but he was hot and tired, and in no mood to quibble. In Hill's quarters, the captain got out his treasured bottle of whiskey. "This may help, sir. I know this place is rather a shock after the Coast, but it grows on you. There's something about the desert, sir, that gets to you."

"I shall try very hard not to discover it," Sykes replied shortly.

Hill reviewed for him the Indian situation. "You have

two men here," he added, "who are invaluable. There's
a Delaware Indian who has scouted for the army, served
in it as he does now, and he is a master at tracking.
The other one is Sergeant Morty Callaghen."

"Sergeant?"

"Yes, sir. I promoted him to sergeant after Lieutenant
Allison was killed. He's a very able man. He knows
the desert better than any white man I know, and after
Allison was killed he took over and led the remnants
of the patrol back out of the desert. I doubt if any other
man could have done so."

"I know the man."

Hill spoke mildly. "Too bad you are losing him. He's
the best man you have."

"I do not intend to lose him."

"His enlistment is up, Major. He is waiting for his papers now. Once he has them, I doubt if he'll remain
long."

Sykes dismissed the subject. "This Allison you mention. He was named in one of your reports, but nobody
at headquarters knows anything about him."

Captain Hill explained as best he could, adding some
of Callaghen's speculations.

"Gold?" Sykes stared at him. "There's gold in this
desert?"

"It's been found from time to time. It's mostly rumor,
I think, but some of the rumors are quite substantial.
The one that intrigues me the most is that of a River of
Gold that is said to flow under the desert."

"Under?"

"Rivers do not last long in the desert, Major. They
sink into the sand and disappear. Perhaps they just evap-
orate, but the story is that there's a river running deep
in a cavern beneath the desert, and that its sand is mixed
with gold. The Indians had stories about a River of the
Golden Sands."

"Nonsense." Even as he said it, Sykes was thoughtful. Supposing . . . just supposing such a story were
true? He was here in the desert. He had ample time
to look around, and an excellent cover for doing so.

And if he found something it would, of course, belong to him.

He dismissed the idea, and thought of more immediate things. In the morning he would go over the lists of provisions, ammunition, and weapons on hand. He would have a look at the riding stock and the pack animals, and learn just what he had to work with.

After he had had his bath he sat and talked with Captain Hill over a drink and a cigar.

"The Mohaves now," Sykes said. "Do you see them often?"

"You only see them when they want you to see them." Hill paused. "You must understand, Major, the Mohave is a different kind of Indian. He is not like the Plains Indians. Not even like the Apaches, with whom he is sometimes grouped. The Mohaves are of the Yuma family, but they are very different indeed."

He took a sip of whiskey. He was going to have to leave it alone. He was getting to like the stuff too much. "When they want to navigate the river they do not make dugouts or birchbark canoes . . . They make boats of reeds, not unlike those of the ancient Egyptians, or the pre-Inca Indians of the Andes.

"They are tall, handsome people, better bred, perhaps, than most Indians. They lack the stately posture and the dignity of the Plains tribes, but the women are often very fine-looking. Their customs, too, are different. I think you will find them interesting."

Sykes glanced at Hill with no particular admiration. "I have never felt that savages were a subject for study. My mission here is to make the road safe for travel. I shall do exactly that. The first time I meet them in battle, I shall wipe them out."

Hill looked at him thoughtfully. "I wish I could stay to see it, Major. It would be a remarkable accomplishment. How many men did you bring with you?"

"Sixty-six, in three under-strength troops."

"Yes, that would be about it. You see, Major, the Mohaves number about three thousand, at the best guess, and I would imagine about seven or eight hundred of them are warriors. Their tactics are different. They are

42	LOUIS L'AMOUR

excellent guerilla fighters, but that is not their way under
ordinary circumstances. They prefer hand-to-hand combat. They want to grapple with their enemies. Sometimes in battle with other Indians they grab them and
drag them into their circle, where they are hacked to
pieces.

"The Mohaves are strong men. They use clubs, knives,
bows and arrows, and a sort of mallet with which they
attack the face with what a prize fighter would call an
uppercut.

"A few days ago when Callaghen was leading back
the remnant of that patrol, the Indians followed on
horseback, but that is rare. The Mohaves prefer to fight
on foot. I believe their reason for following on horseback
in the recent case was to taunt the soldiers, to show them
how easy it was for them, how hard for the soldiers on
foot."

"Yet they were driven off?"

"Largely by Callaghen, from what the Delaware and
Croker said. Callaghen lured them in close, then, according to Croker, who is no admirer of Callaghen, he put
on a display of pistol shooting the like of which Croker
had never seen. No Indian likes to suffer losses, so they
pulled off."

"Very interesting." Sykes was thoughtful. This situation might be different from what he had expected. "What
do you think are my chances for pitched battle with the
lot of them?"

"No good at all. They would have to be quite sure
of a smashing victory before they would put any large
number of men in the field. However, in a war with
the Maricopas and the Pimas they did put some two
hundred warriors in the field, allied with Yavapais, Yumas,
and Apaches."

Hill went to the fire for the coffeepot. "Their arrows
aren't much good at long range, and they don't have many
rifles. One of their preferred methods of fighting is to
charge into a group, grab a man and throw him over
the shoulder for the Mohaves coming up behind to kill.
Often an Indian will throw a man over his shoulder

and those behind will plunge knives into him or beat him to death with clubs.

"You might not think," he added, "that such tactics would work against the guns of the white man, but with a sudden rush they are very effective. When unexpected, they can be disastrous."

Sykes was quiet. A bigoted man he might be, but he was no fool, and he was suddenly aware that the Mohave was something new for him.

"They live along the river?"

"From the Needles north for sixty or seventy miles, I'd say. Naturally, there are no actual boundaries, and any such statement must be elastic. They hunt very little—for one reason, there simply isn't much to hunt. They are farmers, planting on land flooded by the Colorado, as the Egyptians did on land flooded by the Nile. They grow corn, wheat, pumpkins, squash, melons, and a few other things. Mesquite beans are an item of diet that is very important."

"They travel on foot?"

"Preferably. And they can run all day, day after day. They come out of the desert like ghosts, and vanish into it the same way."

Suddenly Sykes was no longer listening, for his thoughts had returned to the strange story of the River of the Golden Sands.

Was there such a river? Could he find it? And if so, could he get the gold out for himself? Without anyone knowing?

CHAPTER 7

Callaghen was a man at home in the desert, which has always been a place of legend and of mystery, a lost world wherein lost mines and lost cities have been found, seen, or speculated about. In the vast emptiness of the desert almost anything could happen.

The desert preserves. What other lands destroy, the desert keeps. It accepts dead things, holds them close, and draws away the rot that would destroy; given time, it mummifies or crystalizes.

If the dead are undisturbed, the sun, the dry air, and the sand take out the moisture and preserve the body. Much of the Egyptian success with mummification was due to the dryness of the air rather than to any secret process. We would know little of the history of the ancient world if so much of it had not happened in arid lands. Callaghen, who knew something of the deserts of the Sahara, Afghanistan, India, and Turkestan, and who had ridden many a desert mile by camel as well as by horse, was prepared to believe that this desert, too, had its mysteries.

But he was wise enough to know that man has no final answers. The knowledge of ancient peoples has merely scratched the surface. Out there in the desert there might be things of which man as yet knows nothing.

At Buffum's saloon in Los Angeles a man had shown him gold nuggets found in the San Gabriel Mountains, and gold-dust washed from its streams. Within a mile of Camp Cady he had picked up pieces of agate, and had found jasper and chalcedony in canyons to the north. Twice he had been shown "rubies" found near a crater in

44

the desert, but the rubies had proved to be garnets . . . attractive stones, but definitely not rubies.

Several times when on patrol in the desert he had crossed Indian trails that went to unknown places. There was Indian writing at a dozen places he had visited—evidence that men had been there.

Once, digging an entrenchment in the desert, he had found a layer of black soil, bu'lt from decayed vegetation at some time when the desert must have been less arid. He had come across the same thing in the Sahara; and on rock walls in the Hoggar he had seen paintings of horse-drawn chariots, giraffes, zebras, and wild cattle . . . all creatures that must have lived there at an earlier time when the climate was much less dry.

Captain Hill was interested in all this. As for himself, his papers would be along soon and then he would leave. He had been thinking of coming back, but he knew that too often other things intervene and such plans come to nothing. If he once left here it was unlikely that he would return. In fact, he dared not. He had seen too many men surrender to the witchery of desert nights, and to the enchantment and mystery of it all. The desert could be a demanding mistress who gave up nothing to a man, but took all, whatever he had to give. Gold . . . and the desert . . . They had been the death of many a good man.

Croker came over to Callaghen and sat down. "Hotter than hell out there," he commented. "Seen the new C.O. yet?"

"No."

"He's testy. Sharp and testy. I think we're in trouble."

Callaghen, irritated that his thoughts had been interrupted, did not respond. Besides, Croker was probably leading up to something, and no matter what it was, he wasn't interested. He did not like the man, nor trust him.

"This here desert now," Croker went on, "has secrets, things a man would give his eyeteeth to know. . . . You given any thought to this Allison? I think he had something on his mind. If you and me knew what it was we might make ourselves a pretty penny. If he wasn't a genuine soldier, he—"

"What gave you that idea?" Callaghen interrupted.

"Come off it. You know there ain't no secrets in the army. Somebody always hears things on the grapevine. The story is that Allison had been an officer all right, but that he came out here to pass himself as a replacement. He knew it would take a month or two for anybody to find out, and meanwhile he'd have a government escort whilst he prowled about looking for whatever it was. No Indians to worry about . . ."

"He made a mistake, didn't he? When a man's time comes, not even the army can protect him."

"You believe that? A man's fated to die at a certain time or place?"

Callaghen shrugged. "No, I don't. It was just a manner of speaking. Usually a man dies when he gets careless." He looked hard at Croker. "And I never get careless, Croker."

The other man laughed, without humor. "Have it your way. Only thing is, I think whatever the lieutenant was after, you know it. And if you go after it, I'll be right on your tail."

"What I'm after, and all I'm after, are my discharge papers and the first stage or freight wagon to Los Angeles."

Croker stared at him, unbelieving, then he snorted and walked away.

Puzzles irritated Callaghen. There was an answer to most things if a man added things up right. The trouble was, you had to have all the pieces, and in this case there was very little on which to make any decision—it was all supposition. He had a map, of course . . . or he had had it. He had sent back the map with those other things that went to the address in Allison's gear. That he had kept a copy of it was his own business.

The normal duties of the camp continued. Callaghen waited impatiently for his discharge, but saw little of Sykes. Major Sykes was studying reports, and was finding nothing to give him pleasure.

Nowhere did he find a report of a major attack by the Indians. There was continual harassment, with hit-and-run attacks, horse-stealing, and sniping, but nowhere was there any indication of the Indians attempting a real battle. The record showed only another difficult kind of army duty. Both now and during previous occupations of the desert posts, there had been disciplinary problems and desertions.

Hot in the summer, cold and windy in the winter, the high desert offered nothing to entice a soldier. There were no towns nearer than San Bernardino or Los Angeles where he might go on leave, and getting to either place required considerable travel time.

Captain Hill's reports he found brief and to the point, but there were notes appended as to tactics, the beliefs of the Indians, their source of food, methods of fishing, and all manner of odds and ends. In spite of himself he found these interesting. Captain Hill had certainly been observant. Though he had never served under General Crook, he understood this was the sort of thing Crook required of his officers. He believed in understanding the enemy. Sykes was not at all sure he agreed, but some of it could be of value in closing off the food supply and bringing the Indians to terms.

He studied Callaghen's report with particular interest. That the man had been an officer was obvious. The report was brief and to the point, and was put together with meticulous skill. The tactics used by the Mohaves, the condition of the water holes, the kind of country over which they marched, the death of Lieutenant Allison— all were told clearly and with no wasted words.

This last matter was going to be a headache. They would want to know who this Allison was, how he came to be there, how he came to be killed, how he happened to be in command of an army patrol?

He took from the file the orders Allison had submitted on his arrival. Everything was in order. Hill certainly could have had no reason to suspect the man was other than he had appeared to be.

There was a brief outline of Allison's military record. Graduated from Virginia Military Academy—well, that could be checked. He had served at two eastern stations far from the frontier, and anyone might have served at those posts during the time Allison claimed he was there.

Both Hill and Callaghen agreed that the man was a soldier, so he must have been one who had left the service not long before . . . or who had been a former Confederate. *A rebel officer . . .* that could be.

Certainly, whatever he had expected to do would have had to be done quickly, for such a trick could not go long undiscovered. Especially as everybody knew that Sykes was about to take over.

Suddenly, he felt a chill. He put the reports down carefully and fumbled in his pocket for a cigar and matches.

Why had the man come here just when Sykes was about to take command? Was it possible, even remotely possible, that Allison was somebody known to him? Somebody who thought Sykes would permit him to stay on?

Sykes sat back in the chair. Who might have such an idea? Who might presume to imagine . . . He must consider this with care, for though the army might be blundering it was often painstaking, and such inquiries could go on indefinitely.

He could think of no young officer—or an older one, for that matter—who would dare such a thing. He had made few friends during his time in service; and, anxious to get to the top, he had cultivated only those likely to be of use to him. There was no one he could think of who would have presumption enough to try to trade on his friendship. The explanation must lie elsewhere.

He stepped to the door of his hut. "Callaghen? May I speak to you?"

When Callaghen had stepped in and saluted, Sykes said, "This is somewhat of a surprise, Sergeant. I had not expected to see you again."

"Yes, sir."

"Callaghen, I shall have to conduct some sort of an investigation into this matter of Lieutenant Allison. I have read your report. Have you anything to add?"

"No, sir."

"Did Allison make any inquiries about the country? I mean, did he ask about specific places? Did he give you any indication as to his reason for this masquerade?"

"None at all, sir. Nothing that I recall."

Sykes toyed with his pen. "You may be sure this was no whim; the move was well planned. You have no clue at all?"

"There was one thing, sir. By inquiry among the men who arrived with him, I learned that he received his orders from some civilian in Los Angeles. They may have been given to this civilian to hold for him. At least, my informant reported that as Allison was about to board the stage that was bringing them here, he was handed an envelope that was the same one Allison turned over to Captain Hill."

Then, Sykes thought, more than one man might have been involved. Despite the fact that he disliked Callaghen, the man was intelligent, and he might come up with some ideas, but further inquiries brought no additional information.

So after Callaghen had departed, Sykes got out his map of the Mohave area and studied the route Allison had pursued. It told him nothing beyond what he already knew—that Allison had gone farther north than he was expected to go, and evidently had not found what he was looking for.

As for Callaghen's discharge, he glanced at it, and then put it in the file. That could wait. The man's time was up, but Sykes had no desire to be rid of him . . . not yet.

Callaghen watched the men policing the area, then went to the horse corrals. Captain Marriott was inspecting the horses. He gestured toward the horses. "Not a bad lot. I hear you have had some stolen?"

"Yes, sir. The Mohaves eat them . . . or trade them. From what I hear, there's always been trouble with horse-stealing. Peg-Leg Smith and Jim Beckworth used to ride with the Indians, steal horses in California, and drive them to Nevada or Arizona to sell or trade."

Marriott was a slender, attractive man of forty-five or

so who gave the appearance of being a competent soldier and a gentleman.

"I understand you're due for discharge, Sergeant," he said now. "We will be sorry to lose you. Experienced men are hard to come by, and you seem to know the desert, from all I can gather."

Callaghen was watching the trail from the west. There was a black dot out there . . . something coming. While he talked with Marriott he kept one eye on the distant object. It was rapidly drawing near, and he soon saw that it was a stage.

Together the two men walked back to the compound where the stage would draw up.

There were five passengers in the stage, two of them women. From the top of the stage two men dropped down, one of them a barrel-chested, burly man with a thick neck and a truculent manner. He glanced at Marriott, then at Callaghen, and walked off toward an olla that hung in the shade, a gourd dipper hanging beside it.

The first man who got out of the stage was a slender, sharp-featured man with black hair and eyes, and a sallow complexion. He glanced around quickly, missing nothing.

Suddenly there came the word, "Morty!"

Callaghen turned sharply. It was Malinda Colton.

CHAPTER 8

"What in God's world—?"

She was aglow with excitement. "Morty! I had no idea—" She turned swiftly. "Aunt Madge! Look, it's Morty Callaghen!"

Madge McDonald held out her hand. "How are you, Sergeant? This is a surprise. We knew that Major Sykes was here, but we had no idea you were here too. Oooh!" she exclaimed. "I forgot! Major Sykes! Morty, how did you ever get into a unit with him again?"

Callaghen glanced toward the headquarters. He shrugged, and explained about his discharge, and said that his time was actually completed.

"But what are you going to do? You surely aren't going back into the army?"

"I haven't decided, Malinda." He looked straight into her eyes. "I have nothing, you know. I'll have to start all over again."

She lifted her chin. "Why not? The West is full of men who are doing just that, and many of them are far less well-equipped than you are. Uncle John is in Nevada. He's bought land there and built a house. He's planning to raise sheep. When you get your discharge you must join us there."

"I might do that."

Suddenly, Major Sykes was there beside them. "Sergeant, I believe you have your duties?"

"Yes, sir. Certainly, sir."

Callaghen did an about-face and walked away, but he was irritated. Not at Sykes, who had a right to speak as he

51

did, but at his bad luck to have Malinda come here at just this time. And she was en route to Nevada!

She had lived much of her life with her Uncle John McDonald, a man whose better world was always just across the horizon. There were many like him, but he was more fortunate than most, for he had married Aunt Madge, who was perfectly willing to cross any horizon by his side.

There was a saying in the West that certain men were men to ride the river with . . . for crossing rivers in flood while on horseback was no job for a tenderfoot. Aunt Madge was a woman to ride the river with. She had just as much eagerness as her husband had to see the other side of the mountain, and she had infinite patience. She also had a certain quiet beauty.

Malinda's father was a diplomat, often stationed where a young daughter without a mother could be a problem. As a result, she had spent much of her time with the McDonalds, and some of their philosophy had rubbed off on her.

The desert sun was setting. The stage would remain here at Camp Cady overnight, and then move on to the next station. It was no trip for women. John McDonald was hardened to the West and to western ways, but sometimes he forgot that frontier traveling was not exactly simple for women, especially for ladies of good breeding.

Callaghen swore softly. If he were free now, he could ride on with them. The trail to Las Vegas, the nearest settlement, was long and difficult, with the danger of attack from Indians. And even at Las Vegas there was no real safety.

After the Mormons abandoned the place in 1857 it had been deserted until a rancher named Gass acquired the water rights at Vegas Springs and moved in. During the war soldiers had been stationed there at what was called Fort Baker. At present there were only a few soldiers—not more than twenty or thirty men at best.

Did he dare leave without his discharge papers? Despite the fact that his time was up, he might legally be considered a deserter if he left without them, or before he was officially released. And he had no doubt that in such a case Major Sykes's disciplinary action would be swift and harsh.

He was cleaning his rifle when he heard footsteps. The man who stopped in front of him had polished boots that were only slightly dusty. He looked up into a sharp, angular face.

"You're Callaghen?"

"That's right."

"You were with Lieutenant Allison when he died, I believe?"

"That's right."

"Did he say anything before he died? Make any statement?"

Morty Callaghen ran a patch through his rifle barrel, studied it in the dim light, and then replied, "My report was completed and turned into the commanding officer. All such information is his to give out as he sees fit."

The man, who obviously did not like it, had a gold piece in his hand. Callaghen gathered up his cleaning materials and stood up.

"That information might be important to me," the man said. He tossed the gold piece in the air and caught it. "That, and where his personal effects are kept."

Callaghen ignored the gold eagle. His contempt for the man was growing, and he liked him less because he was so foolish as to believe he could bribe Callaghen.

"Allison's effects," he replied, "have been sent to his next of kin, as is usual. Also, Allison was not an army officer, but an impostor."

He started to move away, but the man grasped his arm to spin him around.

Callaghen turned swiftly. "Take your hand off my arm," he said, "or I'll break it."

The man jerked his hand away, but his face was harsh with anger. A gun had suddenly appeared in his hand. "You try that," he said, "and I'll kill you!"

Callaghen smiled. "My advice to you is to get out of this camp—to get out and to stay out. As for killing me . . . if you ever try that, I'll take down your pants and give you a spanking in front of the whole camp. You aren't man enough to kill anybody who is facing you."

The man drew himself up. "I am Kurt Wylie!" He threw the name at Callaghen like a whiplash.

Callaghen merely looked at him. "I've heard of you," he said quietly. "Somebody said you killed a couple of drunks."

Wylie reacted as if struck. His hand dropped, and Callaghen's right fist shot out. The punch was short, sharp, and hard.

Wylie's heels flew up and he hit the dust on his shoulder blades, his gun flying from his hand to land a dozen feet away.

Sykes's voice sounded cold and hard, as he came striding across the compound. "Callaghen! What the hell is going on over here?"

He stopped abruptly when he saw Wylie lying in the dust. The light was dim, but there was enough for him to see the gun in the dust.

Callaghen stood at attention. "Sir, this man is somewhat unsteady on his feet. He seems to have fallen down."

"I see."

Sykes stooped and picked up the gun, looking at it with distaste. "You have peculiar friends, Callaghen."

"He is no friend of mine, sir." Then he added, with just a slight note of warning in his tone, "He claims to have been a friend to Allison."

Wylie was trying to get up, shaking his head to clear it. He fell once, then he got up and brushed himself off.

Sykes said to him, "When the stage leaves in the morning, be on it. Until then you are confined to your quarters."

"You can't tell me what to do! I'm not in your blasted army!"

"Beamis!" Sykes's voice rapped out against the stillness. "You are on guard in the compound. There are Indians about. If you see anything moving in the compound, shoot. Do you understand?"

Beamis was pleased. "Yes, sir, I understand. Shall I escort this man to his quarters, sir?"

"If you please."

When they were gone, Sykes took a step nearer to

Callaghen. "Sergeant, come with me. I want to know what happened out here."

In Sykes's quarters, Callaghen told him, without holding anything back, just what had happened. He did not like Sykes, but this was army business, army responsibility, and something was happening here that might lead to serious trouble.

"And did Allison say anything before he died?"

"No, sir. Only that he regretted not following the Delaware's advice, sir."

"What do you know about this man Wylie?"

Callaghen hesitated. "Not very much, really. I believe he's a gambler, sir, but I could not say for sure. He is reported to travel in some bad company, and he has killed three or four men in gun duels. I believe he rather fancies himself in that capacity, sir."

"I see." Sykes looked at him sharply. "And you say he fell down?"

"The light was bad, sir. He made as if to use a gun, and then he seemed to run into something in the dark. The next thing I knew he was lying in the dust."

"That will be all, Callaghen."

Callaghen turned to go, then said, "Sir?"

"Yes?"

"I believe from the description we were given that Kurt Wylie is the man who gave Allison his orders. The men who arrived in company with Allison might be able to say for sure."

Mercer was on duty as a horse guard, and Callaghen went out to him, was challenged, and replied. Standing close to Mercer he asked, "Were you there when the stage arrived? And did you see the man who got off the stage? The dark man with the broken nose?"

"Yes, sir. That's the one, Sergeant, who handed those orders to Lieutenant Allison."

"Thanks, Mercer."

Just before daybreak Callaghen felt somebody touch his shoulder. "Sergeant? I'm Corporal Williams. Lieutenant Sprague is taking out a patrol, and he would like you to accompany him."

He dressed in the dark, gathered his equipment, and hurried to the corrals, where his horse was already saddled. He checked his gear. All around him in the dark, men were mounting their horses. Suddenly he felt someone close beside him. It was the Delaware, Jason Stick-Walker. "We go again," he said. "They say we show them the country, you and me."

The patrol numbered twelve soldiers, Lieutenant Sprague, Corporal Williams, the Delaware, and himself. Sprague was an officer who had come in with Sykes's detachment, a man of forty or so, bearded, tough, and capable. They lined out in a column of twos, Callaghen riding beside Sprague.

"We are to scout the Vegas Springs trail for ten miles," Sprague said, "then swing southeast and join the Government Road from Fort Mohave."

Day came, and it was hot and still. Shadows were at the mouths of the canyons, retreating from the sun as it rose higher.

They saw no tracks. There seemed to have been no movement along the trail in days; but the Mohaves did not use the trail at any time, and other Indians used it seldom. They scouted right and left, looking for sign, but found nothing. Callaghen had not expected they would.

"We are not looking for Indians," Sprague said. "I want to start breaking my men in for desert work, and to get the lay of the land myself."

Near the trail they came on the ruins of several burned-out wagons. "That happened several years ago," said Callaghen, "when Indians ambushed a caravan of freight wagons. The freighters were game, and made a fight of it. The Indians ran off a few horses, and disappeared into the hills."

"Any casualties?"

"Three wounded men; half a dozen wagons were looted and burned, about twenty head of stock were lost. No one knows whether the Mohaves lost anybody or not."

"Will the Indians attack us?"

"No. Not unless there were five or six hundred of them, and this desert will hardly support so many. They'll

watch us, and when we camp they'll stampede our stock
if they can. Otherwise we won't even see them."

He paused. "We can always recruit more men, but they
can not. There are just so many Indians in each tribe,
and when they suffer casualties it is a severe loss. They
won't risk it."

When they stopped to rest their mounts, Callaghen
stepped down. The Delaware came up beside him. "I
think Indians are here," he said. "I think they want the
stage."

Callaghen nodded toward Sprague. "He has his orders,
and they are quite definite."

Within half an hour after turning southeast they cut
an Indian trail—four warriors on foot, traveling northeast
at a good gait. Sprague knew something of tracking, and
he looked at the tracks, glanced off to the northeast, and
continued on. Six miles farther along, when they were
looking for a camping spot, they passed the trail of half a
dozen more warriors, all going northeast at a trot.

Sprague squatted in the sand and chewed on a piece
of stick. He squinted at the sun, and looked off in the
direction they were going. "How old is that trail?" he
asked.

"Two, three hours."

"And to the stage road . . . how far for them?"

"They'll be there now, somewhere along that road. At
least ten of them."

Sprague got out his map and studied it. "The stage will
have an escort . . . part of the way, at least," he said.

Callaghen waited. Sprague was a good man, a solid
man. He knew his duty, but there was nothing in him
that would keep him from exceeding it if he felt called
upon to do so. Callaghen mentally hefted his canteen,
estimating the water.

In the desert water made men vulnerable, and the Mohaves knew that. Sixteen men and their horses require a
lot of water, and the first move of the Indians would be
to deny water to their enemies.

The enlisted men of Sprague's command were armed
with the Spencer .56-.50 carbine with a seven-shot maga-
zine. Each man also carried a Blakeslee cartridge case, a

wooden container covered with leather that carried ten
tubes of cartridges, each one ready to be loaded through a
hole in the butt plate.

In addition, each man carried a Colt .44 six-shooter,
worn on the right side, butt forward. Their sabers, weapons useful in the War Between the States and in European
cavalry charges, but not effective against the American
Indian, had been left in their quarters, to be worn on
dress occasions. They were heavy, and they rattled too
much; against the lances of the Indians they were gen-
erally useless.

Callaghen wore his gun as regulations prescribed, but
he carried another, as regulations did not prescribe, tucked
behind his belt inside his blouse, easily available in case
of need. He wanted a six-shooter where he could get it
into action fast. Also, having come from another unit, he
carried a Henry .44, sixteen-shot rifle. It fired a 216-grain
bullet with a powder charge of 25 grains in a rim-fire
cartridge.

Heat waves shimmered across the desert, and in all
that vast distance, aside from the thin column, nothing
moved but a buzzard swinging in lazy circles, far above.

Shortly after noon, in a canyon mouth that provided
shade, Sprague halted and dismounted his men for a
break. They scattered in the shade along the canyon wall,
two men remaining with the horses.

Sprague lit the stub of a cigar and squinted at the
heat waves. "Damned hard to see through that," he commented, speaking around the cigar as he touched it with a
match. "It distorts everything. Had much experience in
the desert, Callaghen?"

"Yes, sir. A good deal, sir."

"Is it all like this?"

"No, sir. There's some big dunes ahead, and a lot of
cinder cones . . . old volcanic action."

Sprague glanced at him. "I hear you've been an officer?"

"Not in this army, sir."

Sprague shrugged. "In my last command my first sergeant had been a Confederate colonel. Have you seen
much action? I mean aside from out here?"

"Yes, sir. Fourteen, fifteen years of it." He paused. "I'm getting out, and I'm leaving the service. My papers are overdue."

Sprague dusted the ash from his cigar. "Better think it over."

"At eighteen dollars a month? No, sir. I can do better driving stage, or mining. There's not much chance to get ahead, and a man is getting older all the time."

"You're right about that. And there isn't any shortage of officers. The war provided plenty of them."

He looked out over the desert. "A weird place, Sergeant."

"South of here," Callaghen said, "in the Colorado desert, there's a story of a lost ship with a cargo of pearls. Much of that desert is below sea level, and a man can see the old shore line plainly. The story is that a Spanish ship came into the area when it was flooded, but the opening was closed by tidal bores up the Gulf of California, and the ship's crew could not find a way out. Another story is that that same area was the original home of the Aztecs, and that they migrated to Mexico."

"Think there's anything to it?"

"It's all guesswork, but old Spanish documents do tell strange stories. The Spaniards came first, after all, and they saw some things that time has erased, and of course the Indians had stories to tell.

"The *Relaciones*, written by Father Zarate Salmeron, tells of a party of Spanish soldiers who came to a lonely place on the shores of the Gulf of California and found some Asiatics there. Awnings had been set up on the shore near their ships, and they were trading with the Indians. That was about 1538. They implied they had been trading there for years."

Lieutenant Sprague stood up, and Callaghen did likewise. He said, "Deserts breed mystery, and especially such a place as this, which was not always desert."

"You think not?"

"Dig down, Captain, almost anywhere out there, and soon you will strike a layer of black soil—decomposed vegetation. Once this was a green and lovely land, with patches of trees, perhaps even real forest. Our knowledge is like an iceberg: we know a little, but the vast amount we have yet to learn still remains hidden from us." He paused.

"All right," Sprague said. "Mount them, Sergeant."

They saw no Indians; there was no movement but the heat waves. They rode on, swinging farther away from the trail to Vegas Springs. Again they saw tracks . . . four Indians, these headed northwest.

"What do you make of it?" Sprague asked the Delaware.

"They know the stage comes. They will attack."

Lieutenant Sprague drew up sharply, lifting a hand to halt the command. "You think so?"

"Many Indians ride west by north," the Delaware said, "too many Indians. We see fourteen, fifteen. . . . Maybe twice as many ride from elsewhere. I think they do not ride for nothing."

"Callaghen, what's your opinion?"

"I'd have to agree, sir. Whatever an Indian does is apt to be for a reason. We have found the tracks of three parties going northwest. The only thing in that direction is the trail to Vegas Springs—to Las Vegas."

Lieutenant Sprague considered the situation with no pleasure. His orders had been clear. He was to make a sweep through the desert, acquainting himself with the country, giving the Mohaves a show of force, and scouting to see if there was any activity. At the same time their basic mission was to protect travelers on the Government Road, whether to Fort Mohave and the Colorado, or to Vegas Springs.

They had sighted the sign of what they believed to be fourteen or fifteen Indians. Not a large number, certainly. But their number was not a consideraticn, for on the stage there would probably be not more than three or four men and perhaps some women. And if the Delaware and Sergeant Callaghen were correct, other Indians might also be moving to the attack.

Sprague calculated the time the stage would take to arrive at a point where the Indians, following their present line of march, might attack.

He was not eager for battle, but he was not unwilling

to face it if necessary. Sprague was a soldier who believed in accomplishing the mission he set out upon; and if he could, by presenting his force in the vicinity, thus avoid a battle or prevent an attack on the stage, he would be as well pleased.

"Where would you guess they would attempt an attack?" he asked.

Callaghen glanced at the Delaware. "Bitter Springs?"

"I think Bitter Springs. The stage will stop there for water. It is not very good water, but it is water, and the horses will need it."

"How far is it?"

"Possibly twenty-five miles—closer to twenty, I think."

After another brief rest the column turned north.

The Mohave is high desert, 2,000 to 5,000 feet above sea level, except in the 550 square miles or so of Death Valley, where at one point it falls to 282 feet below sea level.

In summer the temperature can reach 134 degrees or more; in hollows, or in the bottom of washes or canyons, it can run as much as 50 degrees higher.

Winter is a different story. Wind sweeps the desert day in and day out; it is often bitterly cold, and there is even snowfall. The snow rarely lasts long, but winter in the Mohave can be brutal punishment.

Vegetation is scattered, but it is of considerable variety; the most usual kinds are the Joshua tree, greasewood, and a variety of cactus. All forms of life in the desert have worked out their own patterns of survival, and some of these are fascinating. Greasewood has a way of poisoning any other plant roots that attempt to encroach on its territory; viewed from the air a desert where greasewood grows may give the impression of an orchard, for the greasewood seems to be spaced in regular patterns.

During the last ice age the Mohave was a land of frequent rains, and there were many streams. The bones of the giant ground sloth, the mammoth, the three-toed horse, and the camel have been found in ancient deposits. Even then men were roaming the desert, stone-age men who did not know the bow and arrow, but hunted with clubs, spears, and the atlatl, or spear-thrower.

Relatively speaking, much of the desert floor is level, broken by dozens of small ridges of bare, serrated rock and occasional outcroppings. Volcanic action is everywhere evident. In one area there are at least two dozen cinder cones, and there are extensive lava flows, which are formidable barriers to travel by any means except on foot. The Mohaves, who know these flows, cross them easily and swiftly.

Here and there are *playas,* the beds of dry lakes, glaring white under the sun, crusted with alkali and salts of various kinds, and after a rain they are often flooded with water. Heat waves distort the appearance of things on the desert, and mirages are frequent, particularly over the *playas.*

Light rays may cause weird distortions in the atmosphere, which acts as a lens in a telescope, making far-off mountains seem close, and turning distant basins into lovely lakes that disappear as one approaches. The mirage is caused by a variation in the density of the air.

As they rode, thoughts of the desert were continually in Callaghen's mind. He bowed his head against the heat. Sweat trickled down his face, stung in the corners of his eyes, and brought the taste of salt to his lips. The horses plodded on, heads swinging with their movement, all their zest taken from them by the heat and the endless miles.

Weird dust devils danced across the *playas* in the distance, the glare of the heat on the desert floor so great that the hot air, rising quickly to let cooler air in below, sucked up dust into whirling cones that danced off across the desert, some of them small, others towering many feet in the hot air above the desert floor.

Callaghen forced himself to be wary. The heat and the miles had dulled his senses, and the men rode wearily in the saddle. Somewhere ahead were the Indians. By now there might be twenty, forty, sixty or more of them, although out here they rarely rode in large numbers because of the difficulty of finding food or water.

The desert was an old story to Callaghen. He had ridden in the Sahara against the Tuaregs, in Afghanistan when he served with Dost Mohammed; and he had experienced brutal desert heat and desert winds that honed and sharpened him for combat. Desert men had always been fighting men when they needed to fight for survival.

The American Indian was a splendid fighting man, but he found himself facing a new kind of enemy, a tough, seeking pioneer, better armed, better fed, and unwilling to surrender or retreat. Indians might kill them, but they continued to come.

The pioneer came not to raid, but to stay. He settled along the streams, built homes, fenced land. He settled at the water holes, and to the Indian it was a new pattern, one the Indian neither understood, nor liked. Many more white men were killed than Indians, but still they came.

The Indian way of fighting was to gather together, to raid, ravage, and disappear, returning to his own people with his spoils or his wounded. Indian battles were many, Indian wars were few.

The detachment was suddenly close to shade. Sprague lifted a hand and the column halted, moving eagerly to the slender line of shade along the wall of lava on their right.

The Delaware left his horse and climbed the lava flow until his head cleared the topmost blocks. He looked around carefully. Wherever he looked, the desert seemed to be empty, but he did not trust it. He never trusted appearances—that was why he was alive.

Callaghen was waiting beside Sprague when the Delaware reported. "I see nothing, but they cannot be far. We must be careful."

Sprague rinsed his mouth with water, holding it there for a minute before swallowing. He desperately wished for more, but he stifled the urge and capped his canteen. He sat down on a block of lava, and wondered at its coolness.

"How far, do you think?" he asked.

Callaghen shrugged. "We've come on well. Perhaps five to seven miles."

The men stretched out in the cool sand. Four were on duty, watching. Sprague was wise, and he kept them watching for only half an hour, then substituted another four.

When they started again the men would march. They might need their horses more later.

Sprague closed his eyes and the lids burned against his eyeballs. What a country to soldier in! Why couldn't he have landed in one of those cushy spots in Virginia or Maryland? Yet even as he asked the question he knew he did not want that. He wanted the frontier. He wanted the gamble, he wanted the action.

He thought he knew how the Mohaves felt. Few if any of them thought of themselves as fighting for their land. They were fighting for glory, for loot, because that was their way. Well, it was his way, too. Years ago, when there was a girl involved, he looked for any way out of being a fighting man, but he had not found one, and now he was glad of it.

He stood up and straightened his back, trying to get some of the stiffness out of it. He wiped his hatband and squinted against the glare. They might be right over there, just beyond the heat waves.

"All right," he said, and glanced at Callaghen. "Form them up and let's move out. We'll march, and save the horses."

He led off himself. Here, the sand was hard and the walking was not bad.

He considered the men behind him. Five were veterans of the War Between the States, four had fought in various commands against Indians. Three were raw recruits who had joined up when their tightened belts ran out of notches and could be tightened no longer. If they lived, they would go home before very long.

Except the Delaware. He had no place to go back to. His people had been scattered and had mixed with other tribes; many had lost their identity.

An hour they marched, then Sprague halted them

again. "Callaghen, mount up and find that road for me. But be careful."

He need not have said it, but he was sending the man on a mission where he might be killed, and he wanted Callaghen to know he cared. And he did care . . . for every man jack of them!

But he had to use a man who would see, would recognize what he saw, and know what to report about it. Sprague was new to this command, and so far he knew of only two men who might do that.

Callaghen stepped into the saddle, stood in the stirrups, and looked around.

"Sir, that rock formation just ahead—I'll scout it for you. It might be a good place to halt the men."

"Do that."

Sprague moved the column toward the rocks as Callaghen rode away.

Callaghen touched his horse on the neck. "Take it easy, boy," he said softly. "I'll need your help."

He hated being out in the open, and when he found a shallow wash he took to it. *A River of Gold!* Well, he could do with some of that.

Somewhere just over the horizon the stage was coming up the road, and in it was the only girl he had ever loved, the only one he had ever wanted for himself. He'd known a few, here and there, and a fine lot they had been, but this one was the one he wanted . . . and he had nothing to offer her—no money, no prospects. All he had was skill with guns, and a knowledge of the ways of fighting men—and a thin chance of living through the next few hours.

Suddenly he saw ahead of him a winding trail, just two wagon tracks across the desert.

And then they came out of the ground like ghosts, gray-brown ghosts, dusty from the sand in which they had been lying. An arrow struck his saddle, glanced up, and missed his face.

There were at least six of them, and they were all around him. He did not waste time in heroics, but slapped the spurs to his horse and got out of there fast.

Another arrow passed him, and a huge Mohave

grabbed at his leg. Callaghen clubbed down with the barrel of his gun, saw the slash of blood across the Indian's head, and the man let go. Then Callaghen was running his horse, all out.

Ahead of him were rocks, and he went into them, but they were there waiting for him. There were only two of them and he took them in fine style, shooting as he went in.

One took a bullet in the chest; the other grabbed him and he felt himself jerked from his horse. Most Mohaves were big men, but this one was a giant.

Callaghen hit the ground and lost his grip on his pistol. He slugged the big Mohave in the wind, but it never even slowed him down. The Indian lunged, and Callaghen stepped in with a left jab, then smashed an overhand right to the nose. The Mohave had never met a boxer before, and it stopped him in his tracks.

Callaghen's hand went for his belt gun. Too late the Mohave saw it slide into sight. He yelled and leaped, but the gun stabbed him with flame and he stopped, eyes wide, then fell forward and Callaghen sprang aside.

He whistled for his horse and it came trotting to him, stirrups flopping. A bullet clipped a rock close to him, and he grabbed for the horse and ran beside it into the shelter of the rocks.

He could hear shots now from the south. The command had been attacked, too. Finding a space between two boulders in the shade, he led his horse into it.

"Stay there," he said quietly. "One of us has got to get out of this."

He slid his rifle from the carbine sling which he had been carrying looped around the pommel of his saddle, contrary to regulations. Now, with it in hand, he knelt behind the rocks, and reloaded the empty chambers of his pistols

The spot was the one the two Indians had occupied, and it was a good one. There was no approach from the rear or from above; the undercut rock gave him both shelter and shade, and a good field of fire in three directions. Moreover, he could look right down the road along which the stage would come.

It was hot out there, and it was going to get hotter.

CHAPTER 9

Nothing moved out there. The sky was without a cloud, the land stirred slightly, leaves moved gently.

He settled down to wait. He had water, and he knew how to be patient. Without patience no man should go into the desert. The rocks wait for the years to change them, the plants wait for the rain. The Indians, too, know how to wait.

Callaghen had learned patience in other deserts, in other lands. He sat still now, just keeping alert and waiting, ready to pick up any movement. The Indians knew where he was, and they would choose their own time. In the meantime, the command had ceased firing, and silence lay upon the desert.

The stage should be along soon, and in the stage was Malinda Colton.

Heat waves shimmered over the sand, blinding him to the near distance. He could see far off, and he could see the sand in front of him, but a few hundred yards away everything was vague and indistinct.

Though his eyes and ears were alert now, his thoughts wandered to the Suleymani Hills and Dost Mohammed. He had been an officer then, in command of a thousand wild Afghan horsemen, who were born to the saddle and were fierce fighters. They preferred the blade to the bullet, and they preferred to ride close.

In those days he had carried three hidden rubies, to buy his way out of trouble, or to build a home somewhere when the fighting was over. He had ridden a Bokharan saddle and worn a green leather belt studded

with jewels. He had lost that belt in a poker game in
Delhi when the fighting was over.

Today he carried the scars of the years, the scars of a
dozen weapons, the memories of fifty battles, a hundred
skirmishes. How long could a man go on? A man needed
a haven away from all the fighting, a place to live, to
love, to raise sons and daughters. A place where the soil
was his, where the trees were his . . . for the time being.
For the trees and soil we take in trust, to pass along to
those who follow us—better, we hope, than when we
found them.

He had always realized that he might die right here;
he had always been aware that the time might come at
any moment. In the spinning of planets and the march
of suns, in the centuries and the milleniums of time, one
man is a small thing, and does not matter very much. It
is how a man lives that matters, and how he dies. A man
can live proudly, and he can die proudly.

Callaghen wiped the sweat from his forehead, gave a
glance at his canteen, but waited.

Were the Indians still out there, he wondered. Or had
they moved away, vanishing into the desert in their usual
silent way?

Something suddenly moved out there, but he held his
fire. He was not the man to shoot at something he did
not see clearly. Even as he watched, his mind went back
to Sykes.

The man disliked him, or perhaps his feeling was even
stronger. Malinda might be a part of the cause, but only
a part. Sykes was one of those men who must feel themselves superior, and his rank gave him that opportunity.
He was not a bad officer; he had that feeling of su-
periority over his men, and felt secure in it.

From the moment he discovered that Callaghen had
been an officer of rank equal to his own, Sykes had re-
sented him. It was not proper, he felt, for an enlisted man
to have such rank, and whenever Sykes issued a command he undoubtedly felt that Callaghen was critical of
him.

He had waited for an opportunity to assert himself in
some fashion, to demonstrate that he was superior, but

that opportunity had not come. Moreover, the sudden reappearance of Malinda had once more made plain that she preferred, or seemed to prefer, Callaghen to Sykes. It was something Sykes could neither admit to himself nor accept.

Now Callaghen dried his palms on his shirt front and took hold of his rifle once more. He would soon be out of this; he would soon be a free man. His discharge was overdue, but mails were always late out here and he thought nothing of that. However, until that discharge was in his hands he remained a soldier, subject to Sykes's orders. Sykes would offer him no breaks, of that he could be sure, but he needed none that Sykes could give.

The command should be coming along soon. His eyes searched the heat waves over the desert, but nothing stirred there. He listened, and heard nothing. Some time had passed since a shot had been fired. The shooting had been followed by a long silence; he had not returned, and they had not come up to him.

He was suddenly startled by a thought that came to him. Suppose he had been abandoned? Suppose they thought he was dead? If they believed that, they might ride on to Bitter Springs, hoping to intercept the stage there rather than on the trail.

In that case he was on his own. He swore softly, but he realized how likely that might be. How far had he ridden, he wondered. Three miles? Four?

The Government Road along which the stage would come was a mail route, adequate reason for keeping it open. He could see the road, but he saw no stage. Suppose it had been attacked before reaching this point?

He shifted his position, trying to see farther down the trail. At that moment a bullet clipped rock near him.

His horse was safe in a cleft in the rock that provided shelter from even ricocheting bullets. He studied the terrain before him, watching for a chance to get at least one of his enemies.

He had a hunch that this lot of Indians were not Mohaves, but Pah-Utes. They often raided in this area, attacked travelers, and made swift forays on the ranches just over the mountains to escape with stolen horses.

Sometimes they were led by white men. It was an old practice to steal horses in California and sell them in Arizona or Nevada, then to steal horses there and drive them to California for sale.

He glanced at the sun. Another hour until sunset. He settled down for a rest. It was unlikely they would try to cross the desert that intervened, for they had no wish to die . . . they would wait for darkness.

Callaghen relaxed, his rifle beside him, pistol ready to hand. The slight overhang protected both him and his horse against attack from above. He could be approached only from the desert in front or sides. He sat facing a crescent moon of rocks, open sand beyond.

He dozed, occasionally awoke to check the desert, dozed again. He saw no movement, heard no shots, or any sound of riders or stage. He was cut off, completely at a loss as to what was happening or had happened.

As he sat, half asleep, half awake, his mind still was busy. Suppose the stage driver had some inkling of an impending attack, and had swung from his prescribed route?

There were areas of soft sand, but much of the surface was firm and the stage might make its own trail. But they would need water for the horses, which meant Bitter Spring or Marl Springs.

A good distance separated these two places, but how much distance he would have to drive would depend on where he left the regular trail. At any rate the stage seemed to have vanished, as had Lieutenant Sprague and the men.

The air became cool, darkness was coming, a star appeared. Callaghen poured half the water from his canteen into the crown of his hat and let his horse drink. He rinsed his own mouth with a tiny bit of water, and swallowed it.

There was a sandy spot where he could ride out from his shelter. At any other place the shoes of his horse striking rock would make a sharp sound that could be heard at considerable distance.

He waited until full darkness, then stepped quickly into the saddle and went out of the gap at a swift pace.

He ran the horse a good fifty yards, but heard no sound.

The Indians were gone. Perhaps they had left hours ago, leaving only one man to pin him down, and now that one, too, had gone. Where?

He rode down the trail toward Camp Cady for two miles but found no tracks of wagon or stage, nor any fresh tracks except those of unshod ponies. The dim light made it almost impossible to see any wheel tracks.

He circled back in the desert toward where he had left the command, skirting a dry lake, white in the vague light of the stars. Several times he paused to listen.

It was eerie, and a haunted feeling came over him. Where was the stage? Where were the Indians? The patrol?

There was nothing anywhere . . . only the night, the desert, and the stars. To the north mountains loomed, the Old Dad range, with which he was totally unfamiliar.

Dark canyons opened before him, but he circled warily away, and his horse seemed pleased that he did. He could feel the spookiness in the muscles of the horse, feel its doubt, its suspicion of the night.

A clump of greasewood had gathered a hill of sand. In its shadow he drew rein, trying to puzzle it out. The stage should have passed him hours ago. The sound of a rifle shot would carry for a good distance out here—well over a mile—but he had heard none from down the trail, and he had seen no tracks to show it had gone north.

Only two possibilities remained. The stage had turned back, or it had left the trail. If it had turned off, the logical direction would be toward Marl Springs. There were three soldiers guarding the redoubt there . . . or there had been.

But what had become of the patrol? He had heard no shooting after the first few minutes, and there was small chance they had been wiped out. To destroy a patrol of the size of the one led by Lieutenant Sprague would not be an easy task.

Nearby the Old Dad Mountains, ragged and sprawling, seemed like mountains on the moon. They would, if he went on along the shore of the soda lake, divide him from the trail the patrol had been following, and he hesitated to ride north around them. Every foot of the way would be a risk. It might be wise to hole up until daybreak, when he could see what he was doing; but travel was usually better in the cool of the night; by day he could be seen as well as see.

He decided he would ride on, find a place somewhere in the Old Dads and wait and see what might happen. He started toward the mountains.

One thing was certain. The stage must leave tracks. It could not sprout wings and vanish. Nor could the patrol.

CHAPTER 10

The sounds of the desert night are small sounds, sounds to which the ears must be attuned. In all men there remains much of the primitive, and after a short time in the desert a man's senses begin to be more active. But he must listen, he must wait, he must give himself time to get the wave length of the desert, and so he becomes aware of desert things around him.

Morty Callaghen had lived in the deserts of the world, and his ears had become alert, something easier there perhaps than anywhere else.

The wind has a sound of its own, and that sound can be different among rocks, greasewood, the Joshua tree, or cacti. Small animals make only faint rustlings, but these too are soon recognized by the ear. A fall of rocks is natural; displaced by the wind or loosened by the alternating heat of the day and cold of night, a stone may fall, a trickle of sand may follow, then silence. A stone dislodged by a foot has a different sound, strange as this may seem—a sharper, more definite sound.

The mountains, too, are not still, but a mountain lives at an infinitely slow pace. It stirs, it creaks, it is growing or coming apart, but all with a slowness incredible to man.

This is a part of the wonder of the wild and empty places. The desert is always waiting. The seeds that fall on the desert and are trampled into the sand do not sprout with the first rain. There must be enough rain, and it must come at the right time; then the seeds will sprout. Some plants leaf out, bloom, and drop both blossoms and leaves in a matter of days.

73

The fluted shape of many cacti is due to the need to offer less surface to the sun, the spines filter sunlight as well, and most cacti have a sort of waxy surface to prevent evaporation.

Callaghen, traveler from a far, green island, had come to love the desert. He waited now in the moonlight, among the scattered rocks and desert plants, knowing that as long as he remained still he would not be seen from any distance. He waited, and he listened. Overhead a bat circled, dived, fluttering about in an endless quest for insects.

On such a night sound carries far. He listened first for sounds close to him, then for those farther out.

At first he heard nothing, nothing at all. He was about to move on when some sound came to him from far off, a regular, continuing sound. The desert normally has no sound like it. Even the sound of the wind has changes.

This was a sound of something moving . . . not exactly dragging, yet not unlike that. He heard it, and then there was silence.

The sound had come from the north, perhaps a little east of north. Callaghen's horse had heard it, too. His ears were up and he was looking in that direction, nostrils flaring for scent.

"We'll go see," Callaghen said softly.

Callaghen's eyes had been picking out ways to move from where he was, and now he chose one of them. He did not mount, not wanting to offer too much of a silhouette to whatever or whoever might be out there, and he did not reach for his carbine, which was slung to the pommel. He would get close enough for a hand gun, and now he unbuttoned a button of his blouse, eased the butt of the gun there toward the opening, and then went ahead.

Deliberately, he chose soft sand. The hard surface nearer by was easier walking, but it made more sound. He followed the route of a tiny desert runoff.

When he had walked perhaps a hundred steps he paused. No sound . . . He waited a moment, and then, scowling, he went on another short distance. . . . He paused again and listened. He heard the sound again, a little clearer now.

Suddenly it came to him. It was the sound of a wagon . . . it might be the stage. If it was the stage, Malinda was on it . . . or she had been. He strained his ears to get the sound of the wheels.

All wheel sounds are not alike. The weight of a wagon and the size of its wheels change the effect. A narrow rim makes a sound different from that of a wider rim; a heavy wagon rumbles. What he had first heard must have been the slide of the wheels when the driver applied brakes going into a wash or down a small slope.

Now he could hear the strike of iron-shod hoofs on stones, the creak of suspension straps. His greatest danger at present was in getting shot, either by Indians, or by somebody on the stage itself who saw him loom suddenly out of the dark.

The stage appeared, the horses climbing first out of a small gully, then the head of the driver followed by the coach. He held his horse's nostrils and waited for the stage to pass. It was moving slowly, and a man was sitting beside the driver, rifle in hand.

When the stage had gone past, Callaghen took his hand from the nostrils of his horse. After a moment the stage reached the top of the small knoll and the driver drew up to rest his horses. Just then Callaghen's horse whinnied.

The man with the rifle turned sharply around, and the driver called, "Who's that?"

Callaghen spoke distinctly. "It's the army, or part of it."

"Come in slow. Keep your hands empty."

Then he heard Malinda speak. "That's Morty! It's Morty!"

He walked up, leading his horse. "Looks to me like you're off your trail," he said mildly. "What happened?"

The driver was Johnny Ridge, whom Callaghen had seen around the camp on several occasions. The man beside him was a stranger.

"Injuns," was the answer. "We spotted them moving to head us off, so when the stage was out of sight behind a mountain we pulled off the trail and tried to circle around, but we got ourselves bogged down and found our way cut off."

"The patrol's somewhere ahead of us," Callaghen said, "but I think your best bet, Ridge, is to follow along the base of the mountain, keeping clear of the sand of the Devil's Playground, until we can find a pass through to the east."

"And how far will that be?" Ridge asked doubtfully.

Callaghen shrugged. "This is no great mountain. There's sure to be a way to the other side."

"But it's further from the Vegas trail, and my horses are about played out."

"You've got Indians behind you, man. Drive on. You can rest your horses farther along. I'll scout ahead for you."

Callaghen went to the coach. Malinda was there, and her aunt, but Kurt Wylie was, too, and the dark man who had come with him to Camp Cady. "You'll be all right," he told Malinda, and rode on ahead.

The mountain lifted two to three thousand feet above them in what seemed to be a solid wall, but these desert ranges were all short, up-thrusts made during some violent time in the earth's building. The Indians would be watching for them . . . by day they would find their tracks, no doubt, and then they would come running.

For three miles Callaghen led the way; then he turned into a cove of the mountain and stopped. Dismounting, he waited for the stage to catch up.

The trail, such as it was, had never been used by a wheeled vehicle before, that was obvious, but Ridge was a hand with the lines and he tooled his team nicely, taking his time.

Wylie was the first man down from the stage. He walked up to Callaghen. "You, is it? I've been wanting to see you."

Ridge turned sharply. "Whatever you've got in mind, forget it. Just now we need all the help we can get."

In a hollow among the rocks, where they were concealed except from someone who stood right above them,

Callaghen put together a small fire. "Have you coffee?" he asked. "It will put everybody's spirits up."

The coffee was produced. The man who had ridden the box brought down a basket and began to prepare food. Malinda came to the fire and stretched her fingers toward it. Aunt Madge moved in briskly, pushing the guard aside. "Leave that to someone who knows how," she said. "You've done a-plenty today."

Ridge squatted on his heels, holding a piece of hardtack in his mouth to soften it. "You know where we are?" he asked.

Callaghen took up a small stick and drew a line to the northeast. "These are the Old Dads. Somewhere over in there is Marl Springs. There should be three or four men at Marl. There's water there, and supplies for emergencies."

"I've heard of it," Ridge said. "I never drove that route."

"When the patrol doesn't find you or me, I think they will turn about and ride to Marl. That was on their route, anyway. With luck, they'll be there when we arrive . . . or shortly after."

"All right," Ridge said, "I'll go along." He thrust a couple of roots into the fire. "You see the Injuns?"

"Swapped some shots," Callaghen said. "I don't know how many there were, but we counted the tracks of a dozen to fifteen before we started over to help you."

"That's a-plenty—more than a-plenty."

Callaghen was tired. He got up and went over to his horse, stripped the saddle from its back and rubbed it with a handful of galleta grass. He held his canteen in his hand, but decided to wait until morning to drink. He led his horse deep into the cove and drove the picket-pin down solidly. When he got back to the fire, the coffee was ready.

The guard, whose name was Becker, gestured toward the food. "Beats army rations, don't it, Sarge? I done my time on them desecrated vegetables, hardtack, and salt pork. In an outfit with a good Company Fund where you can buy extry, it ain't so bad."

The coffee was good. Callaghen held his cup in both

hands, listening to the talk around the camp. He was thinking he had better get some sleep.

Malinda came over to him. "What about your discharge, Mort? Has it come through?"

"It should have," he said. "I expect I'll get it fast enough when it comes. Sykes will want to be rid of me."

"When it does come, what will you do?"

He shrugged. "I've saved a little. I'll have to make a start somewhere. The trouble is, all I know is soldiering."

Malinda put her hand on his sleeve. "Morty Callaghen, that's not true, and you know it. You've handled men, you understand administration, you know something about law . . . there's a lot you could do."

He looked at her, only half believing. He had never been able to decide what to do, once he left the service. He knew a little of too many things, not enough of anything.

"Sarge?" It was Ridge. "Somebody's comin'!"

CHAPTER 11

Instantly there was silence. Overhead the stars hung bright in the black sky, and around them the mountain seemed to crouch, waiting.

Callaghen stepped from the firelight into the darkness, and stood still, listening.

Ridge moved close to him. "I surely heard something out yonder," he said softly. "Heard it clear."

Callaghen heard nothing. Ridge was not a tenderfoot. If he believed he had heard something, that was the way to bet.

They moved farther away from the fire, into the darkness. "Stay close, Ridge. I'll scout around." He hesitated, then added, "Keep an eye on Wylie and his partner. I don't trust them."

"Heard you had a run-in with Wylie."

"So did Major Sykes. He's got something going, but I don't know what it is."

The night was cool. Away from the fire, he saw at once how good their choice for a camp had been. At a distance of perhaps sixty steps only a faint glow was visible, and as he moved away that diminished, then disappeared.

The camp was in a cul-de-sac, a break that notched the wall of the mountain, and was screened by a slight bend in the notch as well as by rocks and brush. It was a spot such as might be found at fifty places within as many square miles, no more unusual than any of the others.

He paused when well out toward the open desert. That sound could well have come from up on the mountain itself. A sure-footed man could cross any part of it, although there would be difficulties here and there.

He expected Indians, and that was the trouble, for the mind must be always open and alert, excluding no possibility.

A curious deer or mountain sheep will not move as does a prowling mountain lion or coyote, and the movements of men are different, too. A white man wears shoes or boots; the hard leather tends to scuff upon rock, to bear down too heavily on dead grass or leaves, in a way which the Indian's soft moccasin does not, and a white man's clothing is likely to make rustling noises in his movements, or against rocks and brush.

Callaghen thought of none of this. He simply listened. He had stopped, as he always did, where his body made no outline against the night, merging with a tall greasewood and a clump of staghorn cactus.

Suddenly, standing alone at the edge of the desert moonlight, silent in the stillness, Callaghen knew it was here he was going to stay. How, he did not know, for around him was desolation, yet a desolation that spoke to him in the softness of the wind, in the bareness of the mountains. But he knew at that moment that he would not leave the desert . . . or leaving, he would return.

He had known deserts before, but somehow it was to this particular desert he wanted to return. Here he wished to stay. Wind stirred the sand out there on the timeless dunes.

He heard it then, some slight sound in the sand . . . then silence. He held himself still, hardly breathing for fear that might blot out a sound he was listening for.

Again it came! Somebody or something was out there. Then he heard a low, shuddering moan, and he left the shadow of the brush with a quick stride.

He saw the man lying on the sand before he reached him, and was still half a dozen yards away when he realized who it was . . . the Delaware! It was The Stick-Walker.

He went to him quickly, stooped and lifted him from the sand, and carried him back to the fire.

"Water," he said to Aunt Madge. "Water first."

There was no sign of a wound, but there was evidence that the Delaware had walked for miles—his shoes were in frightful shape.

Wylie stared at them. "Why would a man go into the desert with shoes like that?"

"His shoes weren't like that," Callaghen replied shortly. "He was riding with me only a short while ago. That's what lava does to shoes. He's crossed the lava beds getting to us."

Aunt Madge touched the Indian's lips with water, and let a drop trickle down his throat. He gasped, and struggled up to his elbow, Callaghen helping. The Delaware took another swallow of water.

He looked around, his eyes staring. Comprehension came suddenly when he saw Callaghen.

"We thought you were dead," he said.

"Where's the command?"

"Gone . . . all gone."

"Killed?"

"I do not know. I don't think so." He looked at Aunt Madge and the others. "We were attacked and took shelter; we returned the fire. . . . After a while one of our men moved. He was killed instantly . . . three arrows, two in his throat. We thought we heard shooting to the north"—he glanced at Callaghen—"that was you, I think."

"I did my share."

The Delaware drank again; then when helped to his feet he walked to the fire where Aunt Madge had prepared some soup.

"I wanted to look for you," he told Callaghen, "but Sprague refused. He had lost enough men, he said, and he must risk no more. Hours passed. There had been shots, but not many. We were not sure if we were pinned down there or not. I volunteered to scout their position, and after a while he let me go.

"There had been at least a dozen Indians . . . all gone. I found cartridge cases from their firing, and I found tracks. They were not mounted.

"I took a chance and went north. I knew I would be

gone longer than Sprague would think necessary, but I wanted to know about you."

"Thanks, *amigo.*"

The Delaware swallowed some of the soup. "I found where you had been," he said, "and I was sure some men had died, but there were no bodies, and there was not you, so I went back to join the command, only it was no longer there. They had vanished . . . there were no tracks."

"Over the rocks behind them?"

"Maybe. . . . I started to skirt the rocks, going the way as I believed they would go, and I came upon the tracks of the stage . . . and of the Indians. So I went into the lava beds.

"There were places to hide there, but no Indians would travel there unless there was no other way. I followed a wash between lava flows, and crossed a wide flow; several times I saw Indians. There were a dozen at first, then four more, then five more.

"I stayed in the lava. There was no way I could get around them to the stage, so I crossed the trail behind them and got into the mountains. The stage had turned along the western face of the mountains, and I came in from the east."

"What about the Indians?" Ridge asked.

"They're out there, you can be sure of that. I do not think they have found where you are, but when morning comes they will."

"We're going to Marl Springs," Callaghen said.

"Then go now. Do not wait until morning."

Callaghen considered, then said, "We'll go back and rest," he said. "We've got five good hours of darkness ahead of us, but the stock needs rest and so do we. We'll start before daylight."

They let the fire die down. All of them stretched out on blankets and slept. Wylie stood watch first, then Becker.

Becker shook Callaghen awake, when the stars were still large in the sky. "Sarge? Time's a-wastin'."

He sat up, pulled on his boots and checked his gun, then rolled his blanket and took it to his horse. In a matter of minutes he was saddled and bridled, ready to go. At the fire he said to Becker, "Wake them up."

There were still coals, and the blackened coffeepot was still hot. He filled a cup, held it in his chilled fingers, and drank. There was no nonsense and no delaying in either Malinda or Aunt Madge—both had lived too much in army camps.

In fifteen minutes they moved out, cautiously, to make no more sound than necessary. Callaghen led off, walking his horse. The Delaware rode inside.

After a few minutes they dipped through a dry wash, came up on the other side, and found a dim trail leading southwest, the one they had followed the evening before along the face of the mountain.

They traveled an hour . . . perhaps four miles at the pace they were taking, and then a gap opened in the range. He dropped back beside Ridge. "Wait here."

He rode ahead swiftly, and when well into the opening he dismounted and struck a light. He found tracks, going and coming, and he had an idea that it was a pass. A little further on he found the tracks of wheeled vehicles.

He rode back to the stage, and it followed him into the pass. On his left the cliff rose steeply for several hundred feet; on the right it was just as high, but not quite so steep.

It was darker in the pass. Callaghen kept well ahead of the sounds of the moving stage so that he could listen, but he heard nothing. The sky overhead was growing gray. Before them loomed a tremendous rock wall, blacking out the sky ahead of them but the trail curved around it, straightening out to a general northeast direction.

He had no idea how far they were from Marl Springs, but it must be at least several hours away. He looked around. The stage was coming on, Ridge tooling his teams over the trail, saving them wherever possible. Callaghen dropped back.

"Want to give them a chance to rest?"

"I'd better." Ridge drew them in, and then as they stood, stamping and blowing, he asked, "We going to have to run for it, Sarge?"

It was light enough to see now, and within minutes

the Indians, if they had not already done so, would find their trail. They had gone about eight miles, and with luck it would take the Indians an hour and a half to come up with them—though less if they cut across the mountains to gamble on heading them off. The Indians were not trail-bound as were the stage and Callaghen himself. Make it two hours to come up with them, for the stage would be moving.

"How far to Marl Springs?" Ridge asked.

Callaghen hesitated, trying to remember all he had heard and what he believed. "Twelve . . . maybe fifteen miles," he answered.

"Then we'll have to fight. All right, let's go."

They moved out, Callaghen scouting well ahead. The coolness of the deeper canyon was behind them and the space between the mountain ridges was widening out. A long, comb-like ridge about four hundred feet high and very steep, cut them off. They must follow the trail around it.

The sun came up, and it grew warm. A quarter of a mile ahead of the stage, Callaghen drew up to rest his mount. The stage was coming on; the Indians might be hidden back in the canyon, if they were coming that way. If they had chosen to cut across the mountain they would have to travel no more than three miles while the stage was doing almost ten. In that case they would be waiting up ahead, where the pass opened out into the desert.

Up there it was no more than three hundred yards wide, and there was a good ridge of hills on their left, offering excellent cover. Straight ahead, beyond the opening of the pass and a few miles of desert, he could see the black of cinder cones rising up.

Once, perhaps a thousand years ago, this had been a volcanic area. There were dozens of those cinder cones, some of them several hundred feet high, each with its crater; most of the craters were blown open on one side.

He waited for the stage to come up to him. The Delaware swung down and walked up to where Callaghen stood with Ridge and Becker. Without pointing, he indicated with a movement of his head the ridge he suspected.

"If they've cut across, that's where they'll be . . . some of them anyway."

"You think some followed us, an' the rest cut over the mountain?" Becker asked.

"Wouldn't you? They must have guessed we're trying for Marl. We need water . . . they know that. And there are—or were—soldiers there."

"All right," Ridge agreed. "I'll stake a claim on that. What do we do? A run-by?"

"Yes . . . and turn sharp at the end of the ridge. The trail will be right back in line with where we now stand, I think. Turn sharp and take them to the main trail."

Callaghen dropped back beside the coach, ignoring Wylie inside. "Keep down," he said to them. "In a few minutes we're going to start a run, and there's liable to be some shooting."

Wylie peered out. "Indians?"

"You won't see them," Callaghen said. "If they're waiting for us, we've got about a mile and a half before anything happens." With a look at Wylie, he added, "If you're any good with that gun of yours, now's the time to show it."

Wylie produced his gun. "I'm good," he said. "You'll see."

The stage started again and Callaghen rode on, not so far ahead this time. He checked his carbine to be sure it was not gripped too tightly by the leather, and opened the flap on his belt gun.

Ridge handled his team perfectly. The grade was slightly uphill. Passing under a looming rock tower on their left, Callaghen glanced up at it. For an instant he found himself looking straight into the eyes of an Indian. The man was a good hundred yards off, but they saw each other at the same instant; then the Indian vanished.

Callaghen allowed the stage to overtake him. "They're here," he said. "They're waiting for us."

His mouth was dry. Ahead of them the pass was still narrow, and the rocks on either side seemed ready to close in on them like the jaws of some primeval monster.

CHAPTER 12

Ridge walked his horses, saving them for the run. Callaghen felt the sweat on his forehead, and he could sense the excitement in the horse he rode. "All right, boy," he said quietly, "easy does it."

At this point the pass widened somewhat, and the cliffs farther back were out of rifle shot. But ahead the pass narrowed again, and for at least a half-mile they would be exposed to fire from the cliffs.

Callaghen looked at them, considered the situation, and decided that the Indians would likely be bunched at the entrance to the narrower passage, hoping to stop or cripple them there, then finish the job before the stage could get around the point and out of range.

Beyond the mouth of the pass he could see those cinder cones, with a black flow of lava at their base. He saw no movement on the cliffs, but he had expected none.

He dried his palms on his shirt front, and pulled his hat down a little lower. They would probably not shoot at him, but wait for the stage to get into the jaws of the trap.

He started to walk his horse a little faster, glanced back and motioned to Ridge. Instantly, Ridge cracked his whip, and the team lunged into their harness and began to run.

Callaghen heard the sharp *spang* of a rifle bullet as it ricocheted from a rock nearby, and then his horse was running. The point of rocks was some distance ahead, but once around it . . . More shots were striking near, and then, suddenly, with a wave of sheer panic he realized

the shooting was simply not heavy enough . . . not enough
Indians were firing.

He pulled in, saw a bullet strike the sand in front of
him and to the right, and then he pulled over to let the
stage come racing up. Running his horse abreast of the
driver's box, he yelled, "Pull wide around the corner!
There's more of them on the other side!"

Ridge raised his whip in acknowledgment, and then
they were racing up to the point of rocks.

The trail turned sharp around it, and the wall of rocks
would cut them off from firing in the pass. But the instant Callaghen had realized that, and knew that there
were too few Indians firing, he had guessed where they
would be: waiting in the rocks for the stage to round the
point and then they would come running right up to them.

He rounded the point just one jump ahead of the stage
and led off into the desert, away from the trail, running
due east.

Leaping and bounding, the stage came after, dodging
boulders and veering around clumps of brush, the mad-
dened horses running with all they had.

Shots rang out behind them, and looking back, Callaghen saw the Indians running from the rocks at the base
of the cliff.

He ran his horse for another quarter of a mile, slowed
to a canter, and then to a walk. The stage rolled up to
him.

Far behind they could see the Indians, and then they
vanished, the color of their bodies becoming one with
the mountainside along which they moved.

Ridge pulled up to let his horses blow. "Good thinkin'
there, Callaghen," he said. "We almost run right into
their trap."

"They'll cut across the mountains, I think. They'll try
to get to Marl ahead of us."

After a minute or two he led off. The desert around
them was empty. To the north he could now see half a
dozen of the cinder cones, and to the south the Kelso
Mountains. The trail ran along the base of the mountains,
and the route they were now taking across the desert

would take them back into the trail a mile or so farther
along.

Callaghen's mouth was dry, his lips were feeling stiff
and sore. He squinted his eyes against the sun, studying
the desert over which they were advancing. Indians could
be anywhere. They had lived long in this country, hunting, raiding, and food-gathering across it in every direction. They knew what possibilities it offered far better
than he did—better than even the Delaware did.

It was a slight upgrade toward the trail, and Ridge
took his time. From the top of the stage he could see well
ahead, and Becker was keeping a sharp eye out for trouble, but no Indians followed them.

"We need that water," Callaghen said to Ridge, "and
they know it."

"What if there's none of our men there?" Becker
wanted to know. "What if somebody pulled the sojer
boys out, an' the Injuns are waitin' instead?"

"Then we'll have some shooting to do," Callaghen replied, and they rode on.

The sun was high now, and the horses were laboring
on the rough desert. Twice they passed through deep
belts of sand; often they bumped and jolted over rocky
areas. The desert was littered with chunks of lava, all the
way from fist size to boulders as large as the stage, blown
out by the violence of the upheaval.

"She must have been hot around here, one time,"
Ridge said, awed by the sight. "Imagine how it must've
been when all those holes were blowin' at once!"

"It might not have happened at one time," Becker said.
"Could have been from time to time, but even so, I'm
glad I'm here now instead of then."

They drove on, and at last the horses bumped over the
last stones and pulled the stage back to the trail once
more. Several miles ahead the trail again cut through a
narrow pass, this time through the Marl Mountains.
Though it seemed unlikely the Indians were there, they
would have to chance the possibility.

It was a narrow, dangerous place, but they evidently
had reached it before the Indians, and they drove through

MEMO FROM LOUIS L'AMOUR

Dear Reader:

Over the years, many people have asked me when a first-rate hardcover collection of my books would become available. Now the people at Bantam Books have made that hope a reality. They've put together a collection of which I am very proud. Fine bindings, handsome design, and a price which I'm pleased to say makes these books an affordable addition to almost everyone's permanent library.

Bantam Books has so much faith in this series that they're making what seems to me is an extraordinary offer. They'll send you Silver Canyon, on a 10-day, free examination basis. Plus they'll send you a free copy of my new Calendar.

Even if you decide for any reason whatever to return Silver Canyon, you may keep the Calendar free of charge and without obligation. Personally, I think you'll be delighted with Silver Canyon and the other volumes in this series.

Sincerely,

Louis L'Amour

Louis L'Amour

P.S. They tell me supplies of the Calendar are limited, so you should order now.

without trouble, and turned right around a point of rocks toward Marl Springs.

The redoubt at Marl Springs was only a few months old. Lieutenant Manuel Eyre, of the 14th Infantry, had directed the building of it; at the time he had been the officer commanding at Camp Cady.

The corral, twenty-four feet on each side, was built of strong cedar logs cut in Cedar Canyon not far from Rock Springs. At each of the opposite corners there was a stone house twelve feet square and just over six feet high. The largest spring issued from a tunnel between the fort and the mountain.*

The redoubt was too close under the mountain for comfort, unless a sentry was kept on the small peak as a lookout. Originally it had been planned to have a sergeant and eight men at this post, but this had rarely been done. To the best of his knowledge there were three or four men holding the position at present. There were several horses in the corral, and as they approached he caught a glimpse of a blue uniform at the gate to the corral.

Callaghen studied the area carefully as they approached, and scanned the country around. He walked his horse on ahead of the stage, a gun ready to his hand.

A man wearing sergeant's stripes came out to greet them. "Ah, Sergeant O'Callaghan is it? Sure 'n' when I last saw you, man, you wore something better than stripes."

"MacBrody? I'm damned if I can believe it's you. I thought you were dead, man—killed in the fighting at the war's end. I saw you go down under three men."

"And if you'd waited you'd have seen me come up with only one, and he didna last long. They were only boys, Morty, good boys but young to the fighting, and I'm afraid they did not live long enough to grow wise in their days."

He looked past Callaghen. "And what is it you have here? A stage?"

_____
* The old holes are now dry. The spring issues from a pipe at the end of the mountain, flowing into a tank cattlemen built.

"Bound for Vegas Springs, but there's been trouble along that route. They'd left the trail, so I brought them here. . . . Any word of Sprague? I'd gone on ahead of his patrol."

"We've seen nobody but skulking Indians, and a-plenty of them to trouble us." He glanced at Callaghen. "We're short-handed here. One man took a horse and left us in the night . . . I hope he made it through, although I'd not say as much in the hearing of the others."

The stage rolled up to the gate, which was opened to allow it through.

"We can use water," Ridge said. "The horses, and all of us."

"There's water here," MacBrody said. "Although it is slow to come, it never stops—at least it never has. But you'll have a drink, all of you, and by daylight the trough should be full again, and the canteens can be filled."

He stopped close to Callaghen. "Is it true about Major Sykes? If it is, you'll be having no good luck."

"It's true, but I'll be paying out soon."

Ridge was helping the women down and Callaghen went over to the stage. Becker walked up to him. "Thanks, friend," he said. "Without you we wouldn't have made it."

MacBrody approached the women. "We've little enough for you, but we'll do our best."

Malinda smiled at him. "Thank you, Sergeant. Whatever you do will be appreciated, and whatever it is will be better than a dry camp out there."

He gave her a quick glance. "Ah, 'tis of the frontier you are? Well, it is better than. The eastern ladies are lovely now, but they expect too much. I will have a couple of the boys rev it up in yonder."

Callaghen looked around the corral. He saw that it was strong, and the water was close. Leaving here might present something of a problem, but they could face that when they came to it.

"How many men do you have?" he asked.

"Three and myself, and one of them the mail carrier,

who should be riding on. They ran him into this place and he's not very anxious to be out again for a while."

"Let him wait. There's nothing in that mailbag that I'd lose a man for."

Four soldiers here . . . the Stick-Walker and himself, Becker, Ridge, Wylie, and his friend. The Indians would not be wise to come against them now—ten men and a good strong stockade, with plenty of water.

"How are you for rations? The usual emergency stuff?"

"No." MacBrody spat. "The train's overdue and we're running short. That's not to say we can't manage a day or two."

Malinda crossed the corral to Callaghen's side. "Mort, will we be able to go on? Tomorrow, I mean?"

"No."

"You think they will still be out there? That they will wait?"

"Why not? The desert can provide them with most of what they need. There is food out there if a man will work hard enough to gather it, and the Mohaves grow food . . . they grow corn, melons, beans, and a lot of other stuff on land flooded by the Colorado. But their hunting, gathering, and planting can't give them guns that will kill at the range of ours, can't provide them with needles as good, clothing as well made . . . so they ride and they raid. The stage represents more wealth to them than several seasons of planting. They will eat the horses, use the harness, trade some of the items in the stage for other things, and will keep some of them.

"When Sir Francis Drake captured a Spanish galleon loaded with gold it meant no more to Elizabethan England than a stagecoach or covered wagon does to these Indians. . . . Drake was a hero to his people, and so will the warrior be who brings back the loot from a wagon train.

"I think you like these people, these Indians."

His eyes looked across the wide valley. Beyond was a range of mountains, sheer rock reaching up for a thousand feet or more. "Like them? I do not know them, but I believe I understand them to some extent. They are fighting men, and one fighting man always has some understanding of another. All down through the pages of history the warrior has been venerated. Only Solomon is respected for his wisdom. Most leaders have been respected for their skill or their success in war. It is the same with the Indian."

"You sound as if you believed in war."

"No . . . I've seen too much of it. But I don't know what to believe. This is a young land, its people love freedom, and by and large they are tolerant; but we must not become tolerant of evil, simply because it exists."

"Do you suppose we could escape at night?" Malinda asked. "Isn't it true that some Indians do not believe in fighting by night?"

"That is true of some. They believe the soul of a man killed at night must wander forever in darkness; but there are skeptics among the Indians as well as among ourselves. I've never paid much attention to such generalities, and it would be just my luck to run into a nonbeliever with a good rifle."

He looked again at the mountain range across the valley, feeling drawn to it by some urge he could not name. It was a rocky ridge, sharp against the sky. He tried to estimate the distance, which was difficult in such clear air. Ten miles? No . . . closer to twenty.

"My uncle will be worried," Malinda said.

"Yes, I know. But one should never expect too much of time. No man who begins a journey knows how it will end. Nor when."

CHAPTER 13

Southwest of the redoubt was a small pocket in the hills where a little grass and brush grew. A trickle of water came out of a hole in the rocks and disappeared into the ground, but its subirrigation kept the grass alive. The pocket was surrounded by low rocky hills.

Under ordinary circumstances there was sufficient grazing there to handle a few horses for a short time, but supply trains brought grain for the stock. As a rule, aside from the horses of the troopers, if they happened to be cavalry, there would be no more than four to six extra horses at the post. Now there were only four besides the one belonging to the mail rider.

Callaghen was sure that the Indians were out there. Those who lurked about the post were there, and those who had followed the stage. At a rough guess, there might be anywhere from fifteen to thirty of them—probably around twenty—and that was too many.

The place was small enough to be easily guarded without undue strain on the personnel, and with the fire power they now had at the redoubt they could stand off an attack. There was water enough to keep them going, but no more than that. The spring produced water constantly, but in small quantity.

MacBrody came over to join Callaghen near the gate. Callaghen explained then, in detail, about Sprague's command and their separation from it. He also added some comment about Wylie.

"Ever hear of the River of Gold?" he asked.

"Who hasn't?" MacBrody said. "By the time you've lived out here as long as I have you've heard a hundred

93

such stories—the Lost Gun-Sight Mine, the Mine With the Iron Door, the lost Ship of the Desert. And I'd lay a bet, me bye, that hundreds of men have lost their lives a-hunting for them."

"I'm sure that's what brings Wylie here."

"Aye. I know the man. It is a bad one he is. I saw him a time or two around Fort Churchill, over Nevada way. He'd killed a man in Virginia City, or somewhere there, and there was a bit of talk about it. I mean he'd given the man small chance, and there was a muttering around that it was murder, but he ran with a tough crowd and nobody wanted to open the ball with them with no more reason than that, and the dead man a stranger."

Callaghen looked around, and felt the desert as a part of him. The afternoon was drawing to a close and the distant sand dunes that banked the mountains across the valley had taken on the rose color of the sunset. The abrupt range rising opposite, lifting a mile above the valley floor, showed a glassy sheen of black under the glancing light. He felt a yearning to go out there, to cross the valley and climb those mountains and disappear into their cool distance. At close hand they would probably not be cool, but that was his impression from here.

But to do such a thing would be the solution to nothing. He was a drifter, a soldier of fortune, or to put it more truthfully, a soldier of misfortune. He had gained little of this world's wealth in his fighting, and that little had been spent. . . . And now there was Malinda.

There was no avoiding the issue. He could solve no problems by disappearing into the mountains; nor could he face his problems any better by re-enlisting. He had entered the army in the first place because there was little else for a young Irishman of good family but no money to do. And for him after his brief meeting with warfare in Ireland, it seemed a logical course.

He had a quick, inventive mind when it came to tactics. Under the right circumstances he might have become a general, but the wars being fought in his time were small, inconsequential ones, allowing little scope for action. He had, literally, followed the way of least resistance. In the service most decisions were made for you, and your food and quarters were supplied; you received an order and you obeyed it to the best of your ability.

He had been a good soldier, some would say an excellent soldier. Moreover, he had risen to the rank of major in two armies, he had successfully coped with the enemy on many fields. But he had never proved himself capable of making a living at any other trade.

He could, it had been suggested, become a peace officer, for until men learned to live together in peace and subdue some of their impulses so that they could live with the benefits of civilization, there must be someone to keep the peace. But that had not been his choice, and he had continued to follow the life of a fighting man.

Now he knew that such a life was not for him—not any longer. It was a dead end . . . it led nowhere.

He could, he supposed, study law, of which he knew a little. That might be a way out, though not a very satisfactory one, and it was one that promised success only after several years . . . If he could only find that River of Gold. . . . But he realized that was just another evasion. He was like those men he had found in every land, men looking for treasure, for lost mines, men who had no other aim in life, and never ceased from looking until they were old and worn and tired out.

His thoughts went back to Sprague. Where was he? Had they found their way back, and did they believe him dead? Had they been ambushed and massacred? He doubted that Sprague was the man to lose his patrol. He was a careful officer who knew something of Indian fighting, and he was considerate of his men.

What was his own duty under the circumstances? Callaghen considered that. Their purpose for being in the desert in the first place was to protect the mail route and those who traveled over it. Well, that was what he had been doing.

Evening had come with its coolness. The stars were out, and the sky was without a cloud. Far away the serrated ridge of the mountains showed a sharp outline.

A fire was burning at the other side of the corral, and he could smell coffee being made. McBrody came over to him. "It is glad I am that you're here, Callaghen. My men are dead tired from the lack of sleep. You can spell us on guard."

"Keep an eye on your horses and ours," Callaghen advised. "I'd not be trusting Wylie and his friend."

The glow of the campfire and the good smell of coffee and of bacon frying were pleasant, but he was uneasy. He knew the Indians were out there, though these might not be of the same band that had attacked him after he left the command.

He had no feeling of enmity for the Indians. They lived their life, a way of life thousands of years old, and he did not think of it as good or bad; it was simply the way things were. They lived according to their needs, the white man according to his—cultures of different backgrounds, cultures each with its own principles.

The philosophy of it all was not important here; here the question was simple: to live or not to live; to fight successfully, or to die. There is a vast difference between the man who contemplates such a question at home beside a warm fire with a drink in his hand or discusses it in academic halls, and the man who faces it on a dark night in a far-off lonely place, with the sweat trickling down his ribs, and savage fighting men closing in on him.

Callaghen moved restlessly around the walls of the redoubt. What would the Indians do? For them, within the walls there was a store of booty. One thing they had working for them, and this was something they had learned very soon. The white man was impatient. He felt the need to move, to be doing. The Indian had learned patience, and he could wait out there in the bleak hills, needing little food, and knowing where there were hidden cisterns of water or seeps that could be uncovered and then covered again, and he could move as he wished.

Callaghen went back to the fire and took the coffee Aunt Madge handed him; then he moved away from the firelight, his eyes blinded from the fire. Looking into the firelight is a comforting thing, conducive to dreams. But it may leave your eyes unaccustomed to darkness, and that is not a good thing in Indian country.

Aunt Madge followed him away from the fire. "You'd best eat something, Mort. I think it will be a long night."

"They're out there."

"I know." She paused. "How many do you think there are?"

"Any number is too many. We aren't looking for a war; we just want to keep the mail route open, and to keep the freight wagons rolling."

Somewhere out in the night darkness a pebble rattled on the rocks. An Indian? Or just a natural stirring in the night?

Aunt Madge went back to the fire. Callaghen walked to a dark corner of the corral and sat down on the tongue of the stagecoach. He sipped his coffee slowly, listening to the sounds from outside the wall—they were few.

One by one the group around the fire left to turn in. His own eyelids were heavy and he got up, throwing out the dregs from his cup.

MacBrody was at the fire, as was Ridge.

"You want to try going on?" Ridge asked.

"We'll wait one day at least." Callaghen glanced at MacBrody. "Will that cut you down much on supplies?"

"We'll work it out, Mort. By that time the freight wagons may be here, or Lieutenant Sprague may show up. And Indians are notional—they might just pull out of their own idea."

Becker had volunteered for the first watch. Sampson, one of MacBrody's men, was assigned to the second. "Wake me," Callaghen said, "and I'll stand the dawn watch myself."

He slept as he always did, waking often, listening for a few minutes, then going back to sleep again. He had lived so long in places where to sleep too soundly might mean death that he had lost the habit. What would it be like, he wondered, to sleep a night through without worry?

The Delaware came to join him on watch. There had been no trouble, but the Indian agreed with him. "They are out there," he said. "They will wait for us to come out."

Together they held the watch until daybreak. Callaghen stared at the hill rising behind the spring. From the top of that hill an Indian could shoot right into the corral.

Well-chosen for water and for other purposes, it was a poorly sited redoubt for defense.

After the sun was up he cleaned his rifle and his pistols, oiling them with care. Malinda came to join him, bringing coffee from the fire. "It was quiet last night," she said.

"The Delaware thinks they will try to wait us out."

"How long will they try that?"

He shrugged. "That is a guess for anybody. Indians are patient. . . . They have to get close to game to make a kill, and they have learned patience. On the other hand, they might take a notion to pull out. If Sprague shows up they will just vanish, I'm sure."

"Mort?"

He looked up. "Mort, have you any idea where that golden river is? Wylie believes you have."

"How do you know that?"

"This is a crowded place. I heard him talking to his friend. He's also been talking to one of the soldiers—the one called Spencer. I think Kurt Wylie knew him from before."

"Thanks," Callaghen said.

The sun came up and the day grew warm. They saw no Indians. Ridge and Becker watered the horses as the trough filled, leading them up one at a time. By noon all of them were watered and the canteens filled; as well as some spare canteens and jars at the redoubt.

Wylie was restless. Callaghen slept some, talked with Malinda and Aunt Madge, and occasionally with Mac-Brody or the Delaware.

Spencer, the trooper who had been seen talking with Wylie, was a tall man, slightly stooped, and he had narrow, shifty eyes. He was watchful and cautious, but he seemed to avoid Wylie.

In the stone cabin over coffee, while Callaghen slept, MacBrody talked to Aunt Madge and Malinda.

"I dinna know him in the old country, but I knew his people. He was an O'Callaghan from Cork . . . there's others in County Clare . . . in Mayo and Tipperary, too, and some of them are kin. His own family lived in a small place, a lovely place near Leap [he pronounced it Lep], a village called Glandore, and a true spot of heaven it is, with a long inlet coming in from the sea.

"Where the water comes in it is like a river's mouth, and there's islands across the opening of it that break the force of any waves. The inlet runs back a few miles into the low green hills, as safe a harbor as one would wish for.

"Many an Irish lad took off from there to go abroad, either to find his education or to go to war with foreign soldiers. Sure, there was little to do at home, with the British permitting no schools, nor any way for a man to advance unless he walked in their steps. I'm not saying the British were a lot of criminals for what they did . . . in their place we might have done the same.

"Mort's family was a good one, and an old one. They kept from the sight of the British, and they lived well and set many a traveler to their table, and many an Irish son returning from the wars, and the bards too. Mort grew up to stories of wars in foreign lands.

"The British dinna often come to the west of Leap in those days. They had a saying, 'Beyond Leap, beyond the law,' and there was something to it, you can believe me. There were some rough lads in those parts, and a Britisher might ride the roads in peace by day, and get his skull bashed once the dark had come.

"Had the times been right, Mort O'Callaghan would have been lord of a manor or a castle, but as it was he flew away with the wild geese, and somewhere along the way he dropped the O from his name and became simply Callaghen.

"You might not think it, ma'am, but he's a finely taught man, with a knowledge of the classics, the law, and much else. He got his grounding in the classics from the hedgerow schools that were taught in the darkness of night with sentries out, a teaching that was without pen or paper, but by the ear only, in most cases."

It was crowded in the small corral, and in the afternoon Ridge, Becker, and Spencer led the horses out to graze on the grass in the hollow. The two stage-company men held the horses on lead ropes while Spencer scanned the hills to watch for Indians. The Delaware and Mac-Brody did the same.

After an hour of grazing in which no Indian was seen, the horses were returned to the corral.

"I don't think they're out there," Wylie grumbled. "I think we're scared for no reason."

"They are out there," the Delaware said quietly, "and some of them are close by. I think some of them can hear what we say."

"Nonsense!" Wylie replied. "There's no sense in our being cooped up here. We could go on."

Callaghen ignored him, but he was wondering just how far Wylie intended to go. And where? And who was he to meet when he got there?

He thought of the copy of the map he himself had . . . what about that? After all, a lost mine belonged to the finder. And even a little of that gold would be enough to buy a ranch or establish himself in some city or town.

It was worth a try.

CHAPTER 14

The sun was hot, and there was not a breath of wind. Overhead the sky was clear and blue; across the valley the black range tantalized him with its unknown possibilities.

They saw no Indians. MacBrody paced the corral irritably. "Where's your lieutenant, Callaghen? Where is he? Where could twelve men disappear to?"

"In this desert?" Wylie remarked. "You could lose an army out there."

"I'd like to have a look from up there," MacBrody said, glancing up at the mountain that rose above them. It was not high, something a man might climb quite easily in a matter of minutes, but there might be Indians up there even now, watching them. A man would be exposed to fire from the rocks around.

"You've got time," Callaghen said. He had been longing for a look from that peak himself, but he hesitated, not liking the thought of climbing up there with Indians around. "Have they ever tried a shot at you from there?" he asked MacBrody.

"Once. Three of us took dead aim at him when he showed himself, and we blew the top of his head off. They ain't tried it since."

Callaghen got a government map from the blockhouse and studied it. It was roughly drawn, but everything seemed to be fairly definitely located. A dotted line indicated the Government Road to the east. It crossed the valley and disappeared into the Mid Hills, through Cedar Canyon. Beyond lay Government Holes and Rock Springs. According to his information, the valley farther along was freely sprinkled with Joshua trees, and beyond that, in the rocky hills, was Fort Piute—or Pah-Ute, as most of the desert men called it.

Mentally, he placed his copy of the Allison map over this one, and it did not fit.

Whoever had drawn the Allison map had drawn everything from some point to the east, looking at the country with no true realization of which was north, east, south, or west . . . or perhaps he had done so deliberately. As no particular point was located, it seemed to him that oral instructions must at one time have accompanied the Allison map.

But the high mountains yonder were located, and also the Mid Hills. Cedar Canyon was not named, nor were the mountains named.

The isolated peak some ten miles to the northeast was clearly indicated, and so were the Kingston Mountains further north. A flat-topped mountain south of Government Holes was also drawn with care, and a spring behind it. Rock Springs was on the map, but no trails were indicated at all.

There were no words on the face of the map, but there was something about the way the pen had been handled that inclined him to believe that had there been words they would have been in Spanish.

It was an old map that Allison had—a very old map.

One thing was obvious. If there was something to be found it must be found somewhere behind those mountains opposite, around Table Mountain, or in the Kingstons far to the north, and that was quite a spread.

"Looking for something?" It was Wylie, who had come up close to him, and was craning his neck to see what he was looking at.

"Studying a way out," Callaghen replied. He nodded toward the east. "We can see quite a bit of the road to Fort Mohave yonder. Once around that mountain, there's a long stretch of open country. After the horses are rested we might make it across there . . . if there aren't some Indians waiting for us in Cedar Canyon."

The trail was not only visible from the redoubt, but from nearby they could see the rarely used trail from

Marl Springs. The trail over which they had come was hidden behind the mountains and they could see nothing in that direction.

"I think we should pull out now," Wylie said. "I'm going to talk to the stage driver. We could stay holed up here the rest of our lives."

"We could," Callaghen agreed mildly. "But I think the first thing is to rest our horses."

Where was Sprague? That question kept bothering him. Suppose the Indians had stampeded their horses? Who was with them who knew the water holes as he had known them when he led his small command out of the desert? Sprague might have a map, but Callaghen knew well enough how unreliable maps can be. Somewhere out there Sprague might be dying of thirst.

Callaghen folded the map and walked over to where MacBrody sat talking to Ridge. "I've got to find Sprague," he said, squatting on his heels beside them. "It just dawned on me that he doesn't have one man who knows this country."

"How would you find them in all *that*?" Ridge asked, gesturing with his right hand.

"You'd never pass the first mile," MacBrody said. "Not even an O'Callaghan could do that."

"Sprague's outfit might give me a lead through their tracks. I can go back where I left them, and trail from there."

MacBrody looked at him sourly. "My duty is here, and I like it that way. I'm looking for nothing out there."

"Don't do it, Sergeant." Ridge spoke emphatically. "You'd have small chance. It would take a ghost to move among those Indians without their knowing it."

"Then I shall be a ghost," Callaghen said.

He squatted there while they discussed his chances, but he was scarcely thinking of their words. He knew what his chances were, but he also remembered his own narrow escape from dying of thirst out there. And he knew where the water holes were. He was no hero, and he did not think of what he was doing as heroic; it was simply that Lieutenant Sprague and his men might need help. With horses they might make it, of course. After all, they

could locate the trail to Marl or Rock Springs, or even to
Bitter Springs.

Sprague and his men were already short of water when
he had left them. If they had not reached a water hole
by now, they were in serious trouble . . . and the Indians
would know, just as they had known about Callaghen and
the others.

"I'll go tonight," he said, "but say nothing about it to
the others."

Ridge dug at the earth between his feet. "Damn it, man,
I'd go with you, but—"

"You're not a soldier. Your job is with that stage."

Callaghen got up and walked to the wall. For a while
he moved from place to place, studying the area outside.
Getting a horse out would be hardest of all, for undoubtedly the Indians would move in closer at night.

There was a restlessness in him that did not come
from their confinement here. He knew it was because of
that discharge which was due, that might even now be at
Camp Cady. He wanted to be free, moving out on his
own, trying himself in the world outside the army.

Men were building a country here. Although some
sought merely quick wealth, others were bringing the law,
bringing order, establishing homes and businesses . . . it
was an exciting time to live. As yet there was no great
wealth; men had only what they could make for themselves with their own strength, their own ingenuity. It was
ability that mattered. Even as he considered that, he was
thinking that even in Europe things were changing. In
England most members of the House of Lords were only
a generation or two away from being commoners.

The old families who had come over with the Con-
queror had declined or disappeared, and many of the
conquered Anglo-Saxons were once again in positions of
trust and importance. The same sort of thing could happen here, and a day might even come when Indians
would hold important positions and direct affairs in the
land they had once lost to an invader.

It was such thoughts that made him restless now, and
gave him that urge to be out and doing . . . that, and some
nameless thing in the desert itself, something that whis-

pered to him with every wind, that stirred with every grain of sand. His mind seemed to wander over such a range of mankind's doings. At this very spring, how many travelers must have stopped! Even prehistoric men who had shaped the flints or the hand axes he had seen; invaders too, who had driven them out. The only law was change, and he wanted to be a part of that change.

Suddenly, Malinda was beside him. "Mort, what are you thinking of?"

"I was wondering about Sprague and those men of his. They must be hunting water now, perhaps dying for it."

"You're going out there?"

"Yes."

"But how can you find them in all that waste? How can you, Mort?"

"I have to try. I'd not forgive myself if I didn't. You stay with the stage. Trust Ridge—he's a good man. So is Sergeant MacBrody."

"MacBrody was talking about your family, Mort."

"Just like an Irishman. He can't keep his mouth shut. There's nothing about my family except that I am an O'Callaghan. In Ireland, at least in some places, that meant quite a lot, but here it only means I am another Irishman."

"It seems as if half the army is Irish. To say nothing of the tracklayers."

"Sure, and tomorrow they will be in politics. Leave it to them. It's the place they can do most with their talk, and the Irish love the sound of words . . . especially from their own tongues."

"You can be one of them."

"I will have to be. If a man is going to take on responsibilities he had better prepare himself to support them."

She said nothing more, standing beside him in the evening coolness that came out from the canyons.

He saw a faint movement among the rocks, a stir of something, and his hand went to his rifle.

An Indian? It seemed unlikely here, so close to the redoubt.

"MacBrody! Ridge!" His hoarse whisper carried across

the corral and he gestured. They came quickly with their guns.

"There's somebody out there, and I am thinking it is one of our men. If he makes a break for it, the Indians will try to kill him. We've got to have a covering fire."

"All right," MacBrody said, and he turned and moved toward his men, speaking softly.

Wylie, Becker, and Champion, the dark man who was Wylie's companion, moved to the walls. Callaghen went to the gate and opened it ever so slightly.

For several minutes nothing happened, and then they saw him.

He dropped from among some rocks, looked quickly right and left, and then began a staggering run for the walls. An arrow hit the ground near him, another flew past. Instantly the men behind the wall opened fire on the rocks, and the arrows ceased.

The man came on, running hard now. Suddenly, when he was almost to the wall, a shot *spanged* in the clear air. The running man staggered and fell.

He started up, a rifle clipped the evening air again, and several rifles from the redoubt fired at the small puff of white smoke above the rocks.

Callaghen lunged through the gate and ran to the fallen man, catching him by one arm and swinging him over his back. Then he ran back, one futile shot smacking the wall beside the gate as he entered.

He lowered the man to the ground, and as he saw him more clearly, he remembered him . . . it was Garrick, one of Sprague's men.

"You . . . we thought . . . you were . . . dead." The wounded man struggled with the words.

"Where's Sprague?"

"Out there." He gestured feebly. "He's . . . he's picked up some lead. . . . They . . . they got Turner . . . drove off our . . . stock."

"Where is he, Garrick? *Where?*"

"North . . . maybe ten, twelve mile." He closed his eyes, breathing heavily. Malinda held a cup to his lips and he swallowed, then paused, gasping. "Peak . . . highest

. . . look at the foot. . . . A lone peak . . . 'way in the open . . . in line with where he is. No . . . no water."

Callaghen got up and walked away a little distance. He knew the place, and it could scarcely be worse. That ten or twelve miles he spoke of was all right out in the open. There was almost no cover. It would be a chancy trip, but he had to do it.

The Delaware joined him. "You know the place?" he asked.

"I've never been there . . . not up close."

"There's water . . . plenty of it, if they have savvy. Three, maybe four springs within a few miles."

"And an Indian sitting on every one of them."

The Delaware shrugged. "I think so."

"The water holes—where would they be from that lone peak?"

The Indian looked at him. "I go with you."

"Like hell. You're all in. Anyway, one man alone has a better chance."

"In open country? Nobody has a chance."

With a small stick he spotted in the sand the locations of the springs from the lone peak. He indicated an isolated butte. "That's Wildcat. You point for that. No matter what, go uphill. The land rises all around in a great circle toward the top of the swell. The peak is at one edge of that rise, right east of it. From what Garrick said, those soldiers are within a mile of water."

"Thanks." Callaghen got up and stretched. "I'll get some sleep." He turned to the Delaware. "Get my horse ready, will you?"

He went into the cabin, got his blankets, and rolled up in a corner.

Malinda watched him go. "Aunt Madge, what is he going to do?"

"You know what he's going to do." Her aunt took up the coffeepot, filled a cup, and handed it to Malinda. "He's the kind of man who will always know what to do, and he will never ask anybody to do it for him."

CHAPTER 15

It was dark and still when he came out into the night. His freshly cleaned rifle, which he held in his left hand, smelled faintly of gun oil; a cup of coffee was in his right.

His horse stood ready, a long-limbed black horse that had seemed the best of the lot. Aside from a small blanket roll behind the saddle he carried a small packet of food in his saddlebags and two canteens.

Only a few stars were showing. The wind was blowing —a not unusual thing in the Mohave Desert—and this was good. It would disguise the small noise he might make in leaving.

The outer gate had been standing open for nearly an hour, with two men watching it. The gate had been opened and ready so as to make as little movement as possible at the moment of departure.

The Delaware ghosted to his side. "The wind . . . it will help," he said as he glanced up where, between wisps of high cloud, a part of the Milky Way was visible. "The Chief's Road," he said. "So it is called by the Crees."

MacBrody was there too. "They'll likely be in bad shape," he said. "You'll be needin' more grub."

"They'll have to do with water. But you be watching for us—if I find them we'll come back." He spoke in low tones. "And watch Wylie. The man's not to be trusted. He's a crook, and worse, and he's a damn fool along with it."

"I will do that," MacBrody replied. "You be carin' for yourself now. It is not good that an O'Callaghan should die out there."

Callaghen handed his cup to Malinda, who had suddenly appeared beside him, and touched her arm gently. "It will be fine to come back," he said, "knowing you are here."

Taking the reins of the horse, he walked through the gate and turned sharply along the wall, keeping close to it in the darker shadow. At the end of the wall he stopped and looked out across the first ground to be covered.

He still had about two hours of darkness before the night was gone, but he did not like the look of the desert out beyond the corner. It was lighter there, and keen eyes might see him. He tried to judge how far an Indian could see in that semidarkness and decided that to see him moving, a man would have to be within thirty or forty yards.

The ground here was gravel, and brush grew spottily. He stepped out softly and led his horse between two clumps of brush, close enough to them to make his outline indistinct. When he had gone fifty yards or so he glanced back. The redoubt was only a spot of blackness against the shadow of the mountain.

He put a boot in the stirrup and swung to the saddle, leaning forward at once to make himself smaller, and then he walked the horse forward carefully.

He saw nothing, heard nothing. Continuing to walk the horse slowly, he kept himself in line with the small isolated peak ahead of him.

The ground rose gradually but steadily. He had crossed this area before, and it stirred his curiosity, arousing questions his limited knowledge of the earth sciences could not solve.

There was here a vast dome, rising from all sides. In approximately four and a half miles the ground rose twelve hundred feet, but at the top there was no peak, not even a knoll. The huge dome was flat, and it was broken by only two or three minor outcroppings. But about a mile or so from the top of the dome there was a jagged peak about five hundred feet high.

It was that peak toward which he was now pointing. Opposite it, near the end of a rugged range of mountains was another peak. At the base of that was where Sprague and his men were believed to be.

He rode carefully, skirting the dome on a wide swing that kept him low enough so that he was not outlined against the sky. At intervals he hesitated, to listen. And always he watched those surest indicators of movement near by—the ears of his horse.

His rifle was slung to his pommel, his pistol ready to hand. If action came it would be at close range. He had gone a mile . . . and then went on another mile. He was walking his horse when suddenly of its own volition its pace quickened. Alert to every move of the horse, he sensed its fear at once. He heard nothing, but he knew there was some danger nearby.

It was out there in the night, and his horse knew it. The animal half turned its head, and he glimpsed the whites of its eyes. It was something coming up behind them, something that made no noise in the night.

There was no wind. He could hear only the movements of his horse, the creak of the saddle. Suddenly the horse shied, and from the ground in front of him a wraith-like figure came up. At that moment something whispered from the other side and he turned sharply.

The turn saved his life, for a thrown club just missed his skull. At the same instant something leaped at him from the other side.

He clubbed his pistol barrel over a skull, and slammed the spurs to his horse. The frightened animal, unaccustomed to such treatment, gave a great bound forward and he felt the clawing hands fall away. He swung the horse at right angles and went up the hill.

They were all around him now, and there must have been a dozen of them. They had been running to meet him, and now they tried to close in. He swung his horse again, driving at one of them, who tried to swing aside, too late.

The big animal charged into him and the man went down, a scream tearing from his throat as he went under the trampling hoofs. And then Callaghen was away, and running.

He heard something—it might have been an arrow—

but he had slipped away from them—it was partly luck, but even more, it was the speed and intelligence of his horse that had saved him.

He did not for a moment believe they would fall back. A good runner can run a horse down . . . all it needs is time, and the Indians had time. He was away for now, but he could not run his horse forever and they would close in—those swift, deadly fighters following after him.

Dimly against the starry sky he could see the peak toward which he was aiming. The dome up which he was now riding went steadily upgrade, and he swung his horse along the side of the slope in a vast, easy circle, going always toward the peak. He scarcely hoped he would confuse his followers—he did not underestimate them, for he knew well enough that they were shrewd, relentless, and ruthless.

He moved his horse into a trot and held it so for a good half-mile. Then he slowed down and walked it up the dome. A dim shadow appeared on his left, another on his right. They were attempting to turn him. But if he turned back, those coming up behind would close in around him.

He drew up and stopped momentarily, listening, then he turned sharply at right angles and started his horse along the slope again at a rapid walk, turning constantly to look to all sides. By now they knew where he was going, and they had no intentions of permitting it. His eyes were accustomed to the darkness, and he could now distinguish the Indians from the Joshua trees . . . if they moved.

Deliberately, he allowed one of them to close in, and when he turned his horse it was at an angle to cross in front of the Indians, trying to maneuver so only one of them could reach him at a time.

The one Indian was close, and Callaghen turned his head away to give him confidence, timing the steps the Indian must make. When he could have taken three steps, Callaghen turned sharply, drew, and fired.

His bullet was perfectly timed, and it was at point-blank range, for the Indian had just set himself to leap. The bullet struck him in the chest, and instantly Callaghen touched his horse with a spur and leaped away. The shot had been intended not simply to kill an Indian, but to alert Sprague that help was coming—such as it was.

He topped out on the dome, a wide-open area around him. He rode toward the rugged ground where the peak rose up above the surrounding country. At the edge of the rocks, he drew up.

He doubted there were Indians here, but he listened for a long moment. Then he walked his horse along the rocks toward the northwest, and crossing the low ridge he drew up again, looking off eastward to the mountain range that edged the sky.

There he waited, every sense alert. The chances were that the Indians would suspect him of having ridden right on toward Sprague and his men, and they might pass by these rocks, or signal to those surrounding the soldiers that he was coming.

The night was cool. Dawn would be coming soon. The mountains over there were a good two miles off and over open ground, scattered with Joshua trees, but offering no real cover.

The soldiers would have heard his shot, and would know something was happening out there in the dark. He waited, the bulk of his horse and himself merging with the towering rock beside him to leave no outline.

He could feel the horse slowly relaxing, the tenseness leaving his muscles. He opened a canteen and took a small swallow, rinsing his mouth before he let the water trickle down his throat. He was tired. The shirt under his uniform jacket was stiff with dust and sweat. He wanted a bath, a good meal, and forty-eight hours of sleep.

He wanted desperately to sleep, but to sleep now meant to die . . . and that could mean death as well for the men out there. He reloaded the empty chamber of his pistol, and stepped down from the saddle, resting a re-assuring hand on the shoulder of his horse.

He must not risk getting killed by his own outfit as he rode in, and he must get those canteens of water to them, and then lead them to the spring that lay due south from here. It was only a mile from where they were—or had been—but a mile in the desert is a long way, and they did not even know the spring was there.

Callaghen scouted the rocks close to him. Already it was vaguely lighter, but he saw nothing . . . nobody.

He sat on a flat rock, his back to the rock wall within a few feet of his horse, and tried to think the situation through.

The Indians knew he was out here somewhere. At first they would believe he was in the rocks somewhere near the soldiers, but they would soon guess by the actions of the soldiers that he was still out here. Very soon they would figure out just about where he was. Then they would tighten their circle and come hunting for him, but they would be scattered out enough so that he must face at least some of them. They would be aiming for a kill.

Riding through them would not be easy, and first they would be trying to kill his horse. They would want him on foot, and also they would be wanting the horse for meat. The time to start was now.

He poured a couple of cupfuls of water into his hat and let the horse drink, just enough to freshen him a bit. He petted the animal and talked to him.

"You and me, boy, we've got to go through them. I'm counting on you."

The black nudged him with his nose, and he gathered the reins and stepped into the saddle.

He looked at the dark saw-toothed range opposite and started his horse down from the rocks. At their base he hesitated a moment, looking out at the deceptively empty-looking space before him.

A few last stars still hung in the sky. A faint coolness touched his cheek as the wind stirred. The twisted Joshua trees thrust their thick arms at him. He spoke softly to his horse. "All right, boy, let's go."

He started to canter. Sitting tall in the saddle, a pistol in his right hand, he rode out into the last dim period before the dawn. His mouth was dry, his heart was beating with heavy throbs. He touched his tongue to his lips, his eyes slanting left and right.

They were waiting for him eagerly, he knew. They wanted him dead, they wanted his guns, they wanted his horse for the meat it would give, and they wanted to stop him from reaching the beleaguered soldiers.

He rode straight into the morning, his gun ready, and death rode with him, almost at his side.

CHAPTER 16

Two miles to go, and then to find where the command had holed up. Callaghen thought they might be of help. If he was attacked there would be shooting, and they might offer supporting fire. All he knew was the report from Garrick, that they were somewhere at the base of the peak before him. If they had not moved.

Now he could see a greater distance. The sky was gray now, and the last star, like a faint distant searchlight, was gone.

There was no sound but that of his horse's hoofs. He started at a canter, covering distance, and riding easy in the saddle. The reins were in his left hand, his drawn pistol in his right.

When he had covered about half a mile there was still nothing in sight. The peak rose high above the surrounding desert, falling steeply, at its base.

He rode on, and then a mile was behind him. His mouth was dry, his heart was thumping. He slowed his horse to a walk, guiding him gently to avoid any possible dips or shallow places on the desert that might conceal an enemy. Another mile to go. It had to be soon.

His view was good now in all directions. He looked at the base of the mountain, at the rocks there. How long would it take to cover that if he had to run for it? Three minutes? Four?

The ground ahead seemed fairly level, with a gentle downward slope until the last quarter of a mile or less.

His mount seemed to tense a little, looking ahead. The ears were up, the nostrils flared. "All right, boy," he said quietly, "we both know. When I ask you to run . . . be ready."

Again, as in the night, they rose out of the desert. One moment the desert was empty, and the next it was alive with them. Early sunlight gleamed on a rifle barrel . . . on another.

His eyes swept the desert around him. One, two . . . four—there were ten of them within sight, moving toward him.

Only two of them had rifles, several had bows, and at least one seemed to be carrying only a club. There were four on his left flank, two on his right; three were ahead, and one some distance off further to the right. It was an open invitation to ride into that gap.

"Uh-uh," he said aloud, "I'll not buy that." But he swung the black that way and walked him a good twenty yards; then suddenly, instead of continuing toward the inviting gap, he turned sharply left and slapped the spurs to the horse. It left the ground in a leap and drove in a plunging run toward the four men straight ahead. At the same moment he fired at the nearest Indian. The man broke pace, stumbled, and went to his knees. A gun roared on his left, an arrow struck the pommel, and then they were all around him. A club was thrown by one of them and missed by inches; another grabbed his pants leg and tried to hack at him with a knife, but missed his stride and fell into the sand. Another Indian leaped to the horse behind him and he smashed an elbow into the Indian's ribs, but a strong arm came over his shoulder and around his throat.

His horse was running all out, frightened and out of control. Callaghen shoved his pistol under his arm and pulled the trigger.

There was a heavy jolt and he felt the arm around his throat loosen. Turning the pistol slightly, he pulled the trigger again, heard a grunt, and the grip at his throat let go and the Indian fell.

With a sharp turn he avoided two Indians rising from the ground and went racing toward the rocks. Shots sounded behind him, and then two Indians came up from the rocks right where he had believed Sprague might be.

But even as they raised up, gunfire came from the rocks and one Indian fell. The other scrambled away, but then lunged for him. Instead of trying to evade him, Callaghen turned his horse and rode him down, the man screaming.

Then he was up among the rocks and he saw a spot of blue in front of him. He leaped the horse over a last circle of rocks and pulled up short in the little cul-de-sac where the soldiers were.

He dropped from the saddle. One quick glance showed him he had come none too soon.

Sprague was propped up against the rocks, his face gray with pain and exhaustion. Three of the others were wounded. One had his head wrapped in a bloody improvised bandage, another had splints on one leg. All were in desperate shape.

Callaghen glanced back at the desert.

The Indians were gone. One body lay out there on the sand. The others had vanished as if they had never been there.

He took a canteen from his horse. "Figured you boys might like a drink," he said.

He held the canteen first for Sprague, whose hands were shaking as he reached out for it. He drank only a swallow. "The rest is for the men," he said hoarsely.

Slowly the canteen went from man to man. "Take it easy," Callaghen said. "Too much of this now is as bad as none."

After all had had a drink Callaghen sat down and asked, "How long has it been?"

"We been out of water two days and two nights," a man said. "They done stole our horses and pinned us down. You sure came when needed."

"We've got to move. More of them will be coming now."

"We're in no shape," Sprague said.

"There's a water hole a mile or so south. We'll have another drink of this, wait a bit, and have another. Then if it's all right with you, sir, we'll move out."

"Any word from Major Sykes?" Sprague asked.

"No, sir. I doubt if he knows any of this is happening, for he's had no word." He explained about the stage, and his own actions. "The Delaware is at the Marl Springs redoubt," he added, "and so is your man Garrick."

He passed the canteen around again and each man took a careful swallow. One by one they began tightening belts, pulling on boots, getting ready for the move. None of them looked forward to it, but none of them wanted to stay here.

Crouched down, Callaghen drew a diagram in the sand. "Here's where we are," he said, pointing. "There's a water hole about here, something like a mile. We should head for that and refill our canteens. Then southwest of there is Cut Spring—another two miles. I think we can make that all right. And we'll have to fight."

"That's the pinch, Sergeant," Sprague said. "We're running short of ammunition."

"I'm carrying a hundred rounds," Callaghen said, "but mine won't fit your guns. I did stick some of your ammunition in my gear, but it won't come to more than five rounds per man."

"That's more than we have," Sprague said. "Two of our men have nothing left. I doubt if there's thirty rounds in the lot of us . . . for rifles, at least."

He sat up. "Beamis, you and Wilmot and Isbel are the best shots. I want each of you to have ten rounds apiece."

"Mercer's as good a shot as me, maybe better," Beamis suggested. "He done some fighting up Minnesota way."

"All right—Mercer too. The rest of you divide up their packs and carry them so you can be free to shoot." Sprague looked around at Callaghen. "Sergeant, we'll need your horse. Will he carry double?"

"He will, sir."

"We have two men who can't walk, so they'll ride. How soon should we move, Sergeant?"

"Right away, sir. It's still cool. I think we can make that first spring before it warms up, and with luck the second. We'd better hole up there through the heat of the day—we can build shade with our coats, sir."

Callaghen led the way, rifle in hand, with Beamis and Mercer behind him. Then the wounded men riding the black, the pack bearers next, and Wilmot and Isbel as rear guard. Sprague marched beside Callaghen, limping from a bruised foot. They saw no Indians on the way.

At the water hole they found no one, although there were fresh moccasin tracks, and here they refilled their canteens. An hour later they started out once more, marching slowly. Again, all the way to Cut Spring, they saw no one. By the time they arrived there the Indians had gone, and it was a good thing.

Callaghen, looking around him, decided he had never seen such a bedraggled lot of soldiers. "We'll keep the horse right close to us," he suggested to Sprague. "If they get him, we'll have played out our hand."

The night was clear after the hot afternoon was gone. The stars were very bright; the desert was still. After a brief fire to make hot soup and coffee, they let the small flame die down and all of them rested.

The spring was among low granite knobs that provided a certain amount of protection. There was another spring some distance off, separated from them by a low hill.

Callaghen slept a little, and when he woke he checked the two sentries, and permitted one of them to turn in. He touched the coffeepot that sat beside the coals. It was still hot.

He filled a cup, moved back to one of the rocks, and settled his back against it. "Heard anything?" he asked Mercer, sitting close by.

"No . . . I surely ain't, but I've got a feelin' they're out there."

"They are." Callaghen agreed, and he sipped his coffee. "What did you do in Minnesota, Mercer?"

"Worked in a mill, as a boy. Then I kep' store. I was doin' fair to middlin' when the massacree came. Little Crow, he went to church in the mornin', all duded up in white man's clothes, then he went home an' put on his paint, an' those Sioux, they turned to an' kilt most ever'-body around.

"They wiped me out, Sergeant. They taken whatever I had an' set fire to the place. Lucky, me an' the wife had stopped by the Larsons' after church, or they'd surely have had us."

"Your wife in Minnesota now?"

"No, she ain't. Those injuns scared her. She taken off back east where she came from, an' I joined up with the army. That was a few years back. I ain't seen or heard from her since."

"Tough."

"Not the way I figure it. A woman should stick by a man, an' up there most of 'em did. Trouble was, I married me a girl who'd never been far from her mama, an' she wasn't up to it, livin' on the frontier, like. I don't blame her, not none at all. I'd taken her to the wrong kind of world. Me, I'd been fetched up on the frontier in Illinois an' Missouri, an' I never knowed anything else."

After a while he went on, "I'd like to go back. I'd like to cut loose from the army an' find me some of this gold they talk about. I'd like to go back there an' show her what I could do. She was forever holdin' up her fancy friends to me. Well, I never had much, but I figure I can make as big tracks as any man.

"I wonder how some of them would have done, raised on sow-belly an' beans the way I was. I had me a nice little store when those Injuns broke out. We always seemed to get along with 'em—I'd of swore they cottoned to me. I'd have bet they wouldn't burn me out."

"When the young bucks get on the warpath they don't stop to think," Callaghen said.

He moved away to keep himself in the shadow. Mercer was a good man, he was thinking, and a good soldier, but like all of them, himself included, he was thinking of gold.

Something seemed to click in his mind at that moment, and he was seeing the map clearly. He was seeing a couple of crosses that could mean an isolated peak, and a series of them that could mean a range. He took a hasty swallow of coffee.

He was on the location of the map right this minute, he was sure. This spot was one of the indicated places; somewhere close by was the River of Golden Sands.

Not much was shown on his map, but in the morning . . . yes, when morning came he would look around.

He had no clear idea why he felt so sure, but suddenly he knew . . . knew he was right where that map had been drawn.

The river had to be not far away. Perhaps north of here.

He finished his cup and threw the dregs into the coals.

CHAPTER 17

Malinda awoke suddenly, the sound of a shot ringing in her ears. Her first thought was of Mort.

Swiftly, she was out of bed and dressing. Half of the room had been curtained off for Aunt Madge and herself, the other half was given over to supplies and ammunition. Sergeant MacBrody had thoughtfully left a guard on duty outside.

Aunt Madge was awake too. "You think it is Callaghen coming back? It is too soon, honey. It may take him days to find them . . . and at least a day to return. It can't be him."

"I guess not." Malinda felt deflated, but not entirely so. It *might* be Mort. And the Indians would surely try to prevent his return, and there would be shooting.

After another minute a second and a third shot followed. These sounded closer . . . right outside, in fact.

Aunt Madge was dressing. "I'll make some coffee for the boys," she said. "They'll be needing it."

Malinda opened the door and stepped out. A soldier was sprawled on the ground, Ridge bending over him. He looked up at her question.

"It's Sampson, ma'am. He started across the yard an' some sharpshootin' Injun cashed him in."

"He's dead?"

"Yes, ma'am, and that ain't all. Spencer deserted in the night, and Wylie and Champion with him, and four horses."

"You mean they got away? Without any trouble?"

MacBrody, who was close to them now, answered. "Well, we heard no shootin'. They must have found some place where the Injuns couldn't watch, or they just had luck. Anyway, they're gone, and with Sampson dead our force is cut right in half. Garrick is in no shape for duty, and Sutton's down with the fever, which leaves the Stick-Walker and me."

Ridge looked at him. "What about me? And Becker?"

"Aw, you're bloody civilians, an' we're here to protect you!"

"And likely the civilians will pull you out of the soup," Ridge commented. "When the shooting starts, you'll see what bloody civilians can do . . . beggin' your pardon, ma'am," Ridge said, glancing at Malinda.

"I can shoot," she said quietly, "and although I'm a civilian I'm an army brat, so I'll be on both your sides. So will Aunt Madge."

Aunt Madge was busy at the fire, and the others were keeping close to the walls, away from the center of the enclosure. Becker, rifle in hand, was watching the peak for a shot.

"Sergeant," Malinda said suddenly, "did you know Morty Callaghen in the old country?" Malinda asked MacBrody.

"No, ma'am, I knew of him. He was an O'Callaghan then. And I notice he writes the name with an 'e' now instead of the 'a.' That sort of thing happens when a man's name is misspelled by some clerk.

"But names have all changed down the years. There's many a Sutton or Chester who was Irish as Paddy's pig in the beginning. There's hardly a man alive whose name hasn't been changed more than once since men first had surnames.

"The Mac on my name means 'the son of,' and the same it is with Fitz, only the Fitz wasn't Irish, it was Norman. And many a man took the name of a clan when he was not of the original family at all."

This was MacBrody on one of his favorite subjects, talking at length, as always.

"Mort now, he was a genuine O'Callaghan, the son of a father who had been a leader of a clan that went back into history for centuries.

"The Irish were a fighting lot and might have whipped

the British a dozen times over if they could have stopped
fighting amongst themselves, but they wouldn't put aside
their old hatreds, and some of them invited the Danes to
help, and a sorry day it was."

"You know a lot of your history, Sergeant," Malinda
said.

"No more than many an Irishman, and not as much as
Mort. It was taught in the darkness by the hedges or old
stone walls, along with a lot of other learning. They were
the only schools we had, and those not permitted if the
law learned of them.

"The O'Callaghans, now, were 'wild geese' who flew
away to the wars in France, Austria, or Spain, and there
was many another. Sometimes they came back, often they
died on foreign fields, and sometimes they married and
stayed abroad, as Mort is likely to do."

"Why do you say that?"

He grinned at her slyly. "Aw now, ma'am, you wouldn't
be foolin' a man, would you? I've seen the look in your
eye, and in his. You can be sure that if he goes back to
the old country it'll be you he has with him."

The day drew on. The sun was hot. No breeze stirred.
The horses were restless, wanting to be out and grazing,
but they dared not risk it. Twice, bullets came into the
corral, and once an arrow, which cut through Ridge's
sleeve as he was crossing to the other stone house.

"I'm worried about McDonald," Aunt Madge said. "It
would be like him to come looking for me."

"He'll not come," Malinda replied. "I think he's wise
enough to stay, and to wait."

Becker watered the horses, waiting for the water to
trickle into the basins, and it was a slow thing, watching
that water. There was little food left, for Spencer, Wylie,
and Champion had managed to carry off a week's rations
for themselves.

"If I could only get a shot at one of them!" Ridge
complained.

"They ain't fools," Becker said dryly. "They ain't there
to get shot."

Nothing moved out there—only the heat waves shim-

mering, only a bee buzzing, the sound adding to the op-
pression of the heat.

Within the stone cabins it was cooler. Garrick opened
his eyes as Malinda came up to his cot. "Is there word?
I mean, from Lieutenant Sprague and them?"

"No."

He closed his eyes for a moment. He was very young,
and his features were gaunt from pain. "They were bad
off . . . mighty bad off."

"Callaghen has gone to them. He took some water."

Ridge came in with a cup of broth. "You want to feed
him, miss? We've got to get some strength into him."

"Of course."

He stood in the shadows just inside the door, looking
out toward the northeast. "Nothing out there," he said.
"But they'd travel by night, anyway."

"Will they make it, Johnny?"

He shrugged. "You said you were army, so you know
what the odds are. Some get back, and some don't." He
paused. "It seems to me we should be hearing from Camp
Cady. Lieutenant Sprague is overdue back there, and
Sykes isn't the man to put up with that. And from what I
hear," he added, "the Major is spoiling for a fight."

Ten miles or so to the east, squatted beside Mexican
Water Spring, Kurt Wylie, Champion, and Spencer were
feeling pleased with themselves. "You were right, Champ,"
Wylie said. "Those Injuns want that fort more than they
want us. Anyway, we got away scot free."

"Looks like it." Champion was more knowing, and less
optimistic. He was quite sure one of the reasons they got
away was because the Indians wanted fewer men at the
post. He was also sure that had they started back toward Camp Cady or on toward where Sprague might be,
they would have been attacked. Their route had led
across the valley toward the east, and that way held no
danger for the Indians. "Let's wait an' see," he added.

Spencer was free of the army, which was what he
wanted. He was a man of less than modest intelligence,
and he had listened eagerly to the glib, easy talk of Wylie.
A possible chance of finding gold was a lure he was

not prepared to resist. He did not like the strict discipline at Marl Springs, or Sergeant MacBrody, who was a tough, no-nonsense man. He was well content to be away.

"We've got to find Callaghen if we can," Wylie said. "I'd bet every dollar I own that he has a copy of that map. Croker thought so, and he surely had the chance."

"You should have gotten a copy from Allison."

"It wasn't that simple." Wylie did not develop the subject, and Champion let it go.

Champion looked around them. The steep slope of Columbia Mountain was to the east, clad with scattered cedar and occasional pines. It tapered off toward the north and there was a saddle over which they might ride into Gold Valley. He took another drink from the spring and got up, wiping the water from his mouth. "No use to set here," he said. "Them Injuns might change their minds."

All three mounted and Champion led the way over the saddle and into the basin beyond. Table Mountain and the Twin Buttes loomed against the skyline some five miles off. Champion looked warily at the flat-topped mountain. The Indians knew it and used it for a lookout, for it lifted over a thousand feet above the surrounding country, higher than anything within miles.

Champion had been at loose ends when he encountered Wylie. He had worked for a while with the Pah-Utes, stealing horses from the ranches and running them back to Nevada to sell, stealing horses there and selling them in California. The fact that he knew the outlaw hangouts in the Kingstons had led Wylie to him.

Wylie had heard of Horsethief Spring, but he wanted to know more, and Champion, who had just spent the last of his horse-stealing money, knew when he had something somebody wanted. He held out for cash, and then when he got a smell of what it was all about, for a piece of the business.

He did not like Wylie. Spencer, big and dumb, he could ignore; Wylie he must watch as one watches a rattler. But somewhere along the line whatever they had was going to belong to Champion. How, he did not know—that remained for the gods of chance to dictate.

Champion had calculated his chances, and several things were in his favor. He was better with a gun than Wylie believed, and he could throw a knife as straight as he could shoot. Moreover, he had a good idea what Wylie was looking for, and possibly more knowledge of it than Wylie had. Wylie had been cagey, and had not told him anything definite, only advancing money to Champion and making large promises. But Allison liked to talk when he had the chance, and Champion proved a good listener.

Champion had heard all the stories—everybody had heard them. The story of the River of Gold he had heard as he had heard many others, but this was different, because one night on one of their horse-stealing forays he had listened to the Indians talking among themselves when they believed him asleep.

They had talked of the killing of some strange white men by their forefathers. Gold had been found among their possessions, gold the Indians knew had come from the cave where the river flowed. From what the Indians said the men killed had been not Spanish, but French . . . and two of them had escaped. The story had been told because one of the Indians had reminded them that they were near the spot.

Dozens of fake maps had been sold to credulous buyers, but one word uttered by Allison had been the tip-off for Champion, a word that would mean nothing to anyone unless he knew something of the location of the cave. From that moment Champion had put aside his doubts.

Allison's map existed, and it was likely that Callaghen had it, or a copy. It was also likely that Wylie had memorized that map.

The basin into which they rode offered no suggestion of man. The mountain walls were stark, there were scattered Joshua trees, and in the east two buttes stood like sentinels by the gap that opened into the larger valley beyond.

Champion saw no tracks, but he was wary of this place. Table Mountain seemed to bar the way on one side. To the south was a high plateau of the Providence Mountains, Wild Horse Canyon, and some rugged terrain where there was a gap through which he had never ridden.

Ahead of them there was a spring. He studied the area and looked at the mountains around. He was definitely uneasy. "I don't like the look of it," he said to Wylie. "Something ain't right."

"You gettin' the wind up?" Wylie asked. "I never saw an emptier place in my life. But this isn't gettin' us any closer to Callaghen and that map!"

"It's a big cave." Champion let his comment fall casually. "All the gold may not be in just one part of it."

Kurt Wylie turned his neck with a certain stiffness, a poised readiness. "What cave are you talkin' about?"

Champion took his plug of tobacco from his pocket and contemplated it gravely. Then he bit off some, rolled it in his jaws, and chewed silently for a few minutes. He spat, and then said, "The cave of the River of Gold. That's what you're huntin', ain't it?"

"Who told you that?"

"A man can figure," Champion said. "That's the most gold anywhere around, and it's somewhere in this country. I've heard," he added, "the Injuns say there's a dozen entrances, and some of them say there's miles of cave under this part of the Mohave."

Wylie was not pleased.

CHAPTER 18

There was no sun in the sky when Callaghen and the others started out and pointed across the long slope of the dome toward Marl Springs. Callaghen took the point position, and led off toward Wildcat Butte.

No Indians showed themselves, and they heard no shots. Callaghen walked steadily. Out on the slope there was no place to stop, no place to hide. Sparse scattered growth there was, but nothing like cover, only the open plain under a vast sky.

Callaghen held a modest pace. The men behind him were in no shape to go faster, and at any time they might be attacked.

Ten or eleven miles . . . between four and five hours if they were lucky. Six would be a fairer estimate, considering the shape they were in.

Callaghen was unshaven and dirty. He desperately wanted a bath and a chance to shave. More than that, he wanted water to drink and hours of sleep. When they had walked for an hour he stopped them for ten minutes, and each man took a drink of water.

"I never thought I'd grow to like that place," Mercer commented, "but right now I'd give five years of my life to see it right there ahead of me."

Callaghen looked around, studying every aspect of the slope. For them to be attacked here, their enemies must approach and be within sight for at least half a mile in any direction.

He had taken his bearings that morning. The rock that looked like a great rounded dome, or stupa, stuck in his mind. It was a natural comparison to make for anyone familiar with India, for the shape was identical. The rocks around it were a natural fortress with many good firing positions and a field of fire on all sides.

It was that stupa-like formation that had given him the idea that the map was deliberately wrong, purposely out of kilter. It was there on the map, not really noticeable, because it was small, but when a man had seen the formation he knew what it was, and he would remember it if he had a mind like Callaghen's.

The real trouble was with the Indians. How could a man go against them? They seemed always to be close by, always to be ready, never wanting a fight they could not win, just coming and going like shadows.

He held no animosity for them. They were fighting men, as he was, and they fought for what they wanted, as he did, and he respected them for it. Being captured by them would be bad, but there were other places he had been where capture would have been no better.

Whoever had drawn that map had done so deliberately, so that if it fell into the wrong hands it would do them no good.

The Indians knew him now. He had killed several of their warriors, and they would want him dead so he could kill no more. At the same time, they were careful not to get too close.

As they approached Marl Springs it looked the same—the stockade, the stone houses, the low mountain rising behind, with the hollow where they had grazed the horses. Smoke rose from the stockade, but no one was in sight.

Sprague looked past him. "Do you think it's safe, Sergeant?"

"I never try to outguess an Indian, sir. They have their own ways of thinking. We've come this far, so we'll go on in."

The gate opened. It was Ridge at the gate, rifle in hand. He looked drawn and exhausted.

"Becker's dead," he said. "They got him last evenin'. He was a damn good man."

"Put that on his grave," Callaghen said. "That's epitaph enough for any man."

Malinda came to the door, staring wide-eyed at him.

He went to her. "I'm back," he said, finding no quick words to say.

"Come in. There's coffee." She faced him. "Mort, you haven't come back to much. There's very little left."

Aunt Madge was lying down inside. It startled him, for he had never seen her lying down before. She sat up when he entered. "I'm sorry, Callaghen," she said. "I just tired out all of a sudden."

He went out, and she could hear Ridge talking to him and Sprague. "Becker saw a deer. We needed grub, so he stepped out with his rifle. We hadn't seen an Injun in a long time. But we should have wondered about that deer. It came down into the hollow where the horses grazed. At first it looked wary, and then it settled down to eating grass.

I think the Indians saw that deer and deliberately moved so it would walk away from them, gradually working it within sight, knowing somebody would be damn fool enough to come after it.

"It was too much for Becker. He had to have a shot. He was just lifting his rifle—he'd got within a couple of hundred feet of it—when three arrows took him in the back."

"How'd you get his body?"

"Oh, he wasn't done for. Becker was always a tough man. He loosed a couple of shots at them, then started back. He almost made it, and whilst the women and Mac-Brody gave me cover, I went after him."

Callaghen was tired, but he wanted to shave. He had been an officer too long in outfits where every officer was supposed to be neat and well groomed at any hour. He heated water, shaved, and combed his hair. He felt better, but he was hungry and he wanted water. He drank from the spring, and the water was cold and pleasant, and he felt refreshed all through his body.

He was thinking that by now Sykes must know something had gone wrong, for Sprague was overdue, and if anyone had come to Camp Cady along the Vegas trail he would have learned the stage had not arrived.

Sprague's small command had been whittled down. Spencer had deserted, and possibly had escaped with

Wylie and Champion. Sampson was dead, and Becker was dead. Sutton had recovered from his fever and was moving about, although he was weak. Garrick seemed to get no better.

Guarded by four men, the horses were taken out to graze, and no Indians appeared. Perhaps they were willing for the horses to be kept in good shape . . . they intended to eat them soon.

Seated near the wall, Callaghen tried to focus his thoughts on their problem. Lieutenant Sprague sat near him. The officer had aged considerably in the past few days. Losing good men had hit him hard.

"We will have to kill a horse," Sprague said, suddenly. "There's not food enough for another day."

"Let's wait." The thought of killing a horse did not appeal to Callaghen . . . nor to Sprague.

When the horses were once more within the stockade, all was quiet. Callaghen went into the stone house to look at Garrick. He was sleeping or in a coma, he could not tell which. His breathing was ragged, and Callaghen did not like the look of him.

Ridge was waiting for him when he emerged. "Sergeant, I've been thinking. The horses are rested, and they've done better than any of us. I think I'll hitch up, take the women, and make a run for it."

He lit the stub of a cigar. "Look at it this way. If the women are willing, and I could make it, there'd be three mouths less and it would be easier all around.

"We could harness up at night. I've been studying a map MacBrody drew for me, and once I hit that road no Indian is going to catch me. They were ready for us out there on the route we always travel, but this time they won't be waiting and won't be able to get word ahead to stop me. I think I can make it to Fort Mohave. "I'll need one man to fight them off whilst I drive. I'd like it to be you or the Stick-Walker."

"Have you talked to Mrs. McDonald?"

"They'd like to go. They feel they are a burden here," and they think we can make it."

The more Callaghen thought of it, the better he liked the idea. There was no telling what would happen here.

Unless relief came soon there would be starvation within
the stockade. The men had all been on short rations for
days. With the stagecoach gone, they would have more
room to move, and there would be fewer horses to watch
and to feed. But could they make it?

Callaghen went to Lieutenant Sprague, who was sitting
on the edge of a cot, figuring on a small notebook. As
briefly as possible Callaghen explained. "And he would
like one man, sir."

Sprague studied the matter, chewing on his pencil. He
gestured at the pad. "I've been studying the rations and
what ammunition we have. We are in a bad way, Sergeant."

"Yes, sir."

"What do you think of their chances?"

"Very good, sir. I do not think the Indians would suspect anything of the kind, and they'd have a running start."

"They want to try to get back to the Vegas road?"

"Yes, sir."

"I think this road would be better. Get the stage to
Fort Mohave and let them provide an escort for the stage
on the road to Vegas from there. I doubt if Ridge could
get over the desert to the Vegas road fast enough."

"You may be right, sir. I would suggest, if the Lieutenant will permit, that Private Jason Stick-Walker, the
Delaware, be assigned to the stage. He's a reliable
man, and knows this desert as well as anyone."

"You tell Ridge he has my permission to go, if the
ladies wish to make the attempt." He considered a moment, and then added, "But one man is not enough. Why
don't you go yourself? Sergeant MacBrody is here, and
I'll have other good men beside me."

After hesitating, he went on, "Callaghen, your discharge is overdue. I think you should go . . . and take
Beamis."

"Beamis, sir?"

"Yes. He was newly married when he joined, Sergeant.
He might get out of this alive."

"Major Sykes will be coming along, Lieutenant. By
now he knows something is seriously wrong."

"Perhaps. But Sergeant, take Beamis and go. Try for

Fort Mohave. I think Ridge himself favors that route.
You'll have to run for it."

"Yes, sir. I know, sir."

At Camp Cady there was shade beneath the trees. The
air was hot and still except where that shade offered an
island of suggested coolness. Major Sykes mopped the
sweat from his face and swore softly when he saw that
the sweat from his writing hand had ruined the report he
was preparing.

Captain Marriott stood in the door. "Sir, there's still
no report. No mail has come through from either Vegas
or Fort Mohave."

"Sprague will investigate, Captain. He's a competent
man."

"He may have run into trouble, sir."

Sykes put down his pen. The heat had made him ir-
ritable, but he stifled the feeling. Marriott was a good
man, and whatever he himself accomplished out here
would be due in great measure to the kind of men who
served him.

"You may be right," he said, and walked to the door.
Maybe this was his chance. At any rate it was an excuse
to take the men into the field. If he could pin down the
Mohaves . . .

It was abominably hot, but if they traveled early and
late, resting through the heat of the daytime, they could
make good time and save the horses.

"All right, Marriott. We'll take three men and a pack
train. Rations for three weeks. We will march to Marl
Springs, eastward to Rock Spring and Fort Piute, and
if necessary to the Indian villages on the Colorado."

Marriott thought of the discharge, pigeon-holed in
Sykes's desk. "Sergeant Callaghen is out there, sir."

"Oh, yes. So he is."

Marriott hesitated a moment, then went about his business. Callaghen wanted that discharge badly, and Sykes
knew it, and in all justice he should deliver it to him.
However, if Sykes wanted Callaghen to return here it was
Sykes's business, except . . . Marriott frowned. Sykes had
had the discharge *before* Callaghen left the post.

There was much to do. Captain Marriott was a man
who knew his men and delegated authority well, but on
this occasion he personally checked every horse, walking
among them, making certain they were in the best of
shape, and talking to the riders. A desert campaign is
fiercely demanding, and Marriott was uneasy. His every
instinct told him there was trouble out there, or the
others would have been back. Sprague was a good man,
and he had good men with him.

He checked the supply list, and after that he returned
to his quarters to write letters. Several times his thoughts
returned to Callaghen. He had liked the man—a good,
solid man . . . and that girl . . . there was something going
on there, all right.

If they were still alive . . .

The morning was clear and bright when the command
moved out from Camp Cady. Major Sykes, on a fine
chestnut horse, rode in the van, preceded only by two
scouts.

The route he had chosen would follow the Mohave
River, for the water it would provide. And that route
would take them through Cave Canyon.

Major Sykes had never entered Cave Canyon. He simply knew that it was the route followed by Jedediah
Smith, by Frémont, and others . . . therefore a good
route.

The bed of the Mohave River as it left the Camp Cady
area was broad and sandy. It was easy traveling, and the
two troops moved out with confidence.

CHAPTER 19

At Marl Springs the night was dark. A slight wind was blowing, and against the skyline the rugged mountains at which Callaghen had so often gazed stood out sharply against the sky.

From his freshly cleaned rifle he could smell the gun oil as he stood in the open gate, looking out into the night. In a few minutes the stage would roll through that gate and move out toward the Government Road to Rock Springs.

Ahead lay that long sweep of open country across the valley toward the Mid Hills. By day they would have been completely exposed, but at night there was a chance. Whether these Indians preferred fighting by day, as did their friends the Apaches, Callaghen did not know; he only knew that by night they seemed less vigilent.

He heard the creak of the stage as Aunt Madge and Malinda got in, but he did not turn his head as he watched the area outside.

Callaghen would go, and with him the Stick-Walker and Beamis, as Lieutenant Sprague had decided. Their mission would be to guard the stage and, if possible, to give help to the beleaguered station.

Sprague came to the gate. He held out his hand to Callaghen. "Luck go with you. You'll need it."

"And luck to you, Lieutenant. It has been a pleasure serving with you."

Sprague smiled wryly. "Has it? We've had nothing but trouble, Sergeant."

"We expected that when we joined up." He paused.

"I'll get them through, Lieutenant, and then I'll come back."

"You'll do no such thing!" Sprague spoke roughly. "Don't be a damn fool, Callaghen. You're out of it— your discharge is due. You stay with that girl. Anyway, we'll have relief before you could get back . . . or it will be too late to do us any good."

They stood silent, and Ridge came to them. "We're ready, Lieutenant. Sergeant, are you riding inside?"

"No, I'll keep my horse."

"All right. I'll take the Delaware on the box with me, and let Beamis ride inside with the women. He's a good lad, and he'll reassure them."

Callaghen chuckled. "Reassure Aunt Madge? Ridge, you're joking. That woman is tougher than any one of us. She's got *sand*."

Ridge shrugged. "All right," he said. "Let's go."

Callaghen went to his horse and stepped into the saddle. He lifted a hand in salute to the Lieutenant, then led the way through the gate.

All was quiet; there was only the stirring of the wind, only the odd moan of it through the Joshua leaves. He kept to the sand, and the stage rocked and rolled after him, moving slowly. Nothing else moved. The twin ruts of the trail showed white before them as they moved into the trail.

They went ahead almost silently. He could hear the creak of the stage springs and an occasional rattle of harness, but nothing else. Out on the road he moved into a canter, and behind him Ridge shook his lines and the horses began to trot.

They were well away, and whatever happened now, they were committed.

The minutes went by . . . nothing happened.

When an hour had passed, Ridge drew up to rest his horses and Callaghen rode back beside the stage. "Are you all right?" he asked.

"Yes. Is the worst over?" Malinda wanted to know.

"Not until we get to Fort Mohave. We've gotten out without their hearing, or else they've been willing to let us go. Really, it is the station they want. They believe there's more there than there is."

Then for another hour they moved steadily, walking the horses, with frequent stops to rest them and to listen. During all this time they saw nothing in the night around them, heard no sound; but off to the south they could make out the strange white gleam of the great dunes that banked the mountains, ahead of them the ridge of the Mid Hills.

It was past midnight now. Callaghen rode back to the stage again and drew up where he could talk in low tones. "We've been climbing the last two, three miles. Right ahead is Cedar Canyon. It's narrow, and the road winds more than two miles through the canyon, every bit of it a danger. So sit tight."

Beamis spoke up. "You think there'll be Indians?"

"Maybe. You keep your gun handy, Beamis."

One of the horses stamped on the hard road. The stars were bright, and the Joshua trees flung their wild arms to the sky.

"If we get through the canyon it's a nice run to the Government Holes. Usually there's water there, but if there isn't, there's Rock Springs right beyond. There's too much cover there for safety, too much chance of an ambush. We'd have to stop short and one man would have to go for water."

"I'll go," Beamis said.

They waited there a moment more in the cool wind. Starlight glanced along the polished rock of the mountain's face a few miles south—just a black shine above the white of the sands.

"All right, Sarge?" That was Ridge.

"Let 'er roll."

The Delaware looked at him. "I smell trouble," he said. "I do not like this place, this Cedar Canyon."

The stage started on, and Callaghen rode on the left side of it, keeping pace with the window where Malinda sat. It was good to be that close to her.

Now they were in the canyon itself, with only the sky overhead. The sides of the canyon rose up steeply. By the time they had rounded the second turn they could smell the cedars.

The trail narrowed. The horses were pulling well. Callaghen rode forward, but he had not passed the driver's seat when there was a crashing volley and something struck him alongside the head. He felt himself falling, grabbed wildly, and held briefly as he fell clear. Then he hit ground, lost his hold, and darkness rolled over him.

It was cold. He was lying on the hard ground, lying on stones. He opened his eyes slowly and saw a sky faintly gray-blue, with only a few stars remaining.

He lay perfectly still, not yet fully aware of things. Then it returned to him—the sudden firing, falling . . . He started to move, and felt a throb of pain in his skull. He lay still then, gathering strength to try again.

He could hear nothing in the night. Slowly, more carefully this time, he sat up. It hurt, but he made it.

The stage was gone. A dozen yards away lay the body of a man sprawled on the road.

He got up, felt for his gun. It was there. His shirt had been ripped open. He touched his pocket where he had put the map, and it was gone. No matter . . . he didn't need it, and unless they could read it right it would do them no good.

He succeeded in getting to his feet, and looked around for his rifle. It did not seem to be there.

He went to the body and turned the man over. It was Ridge. He'd been hit at least twice through the lungs.

There was no sign of Beamis—he must still be with the stage then . . . but what of the Delaware? He was gone, too.

Callaghen's head throbbed with a dull, heavy ache that made him wrinkle his forehead against it. Weaving slightly, he walked away from Ridge's body and looked down at the ground.

The tracks of the stage were there, tracks of some horses, and the tracks of two feet, side by side, deep in the loose earth on the trail. Callaghen considered those tracks. He was only an average tracker, but those footprints . . . Somebody had jumped from the stage, landing on both feet.

Scouting, he picked up one more track. The man, whoever he was, had ducked into the rocks and cedars near
the trail. It was poor cover, but for a man who knew how
to use it, it might do. It was probably the Delaware, and
there was a good chance he had gotten away, and would
be trailing the stage.

With the growing light he suddenly saw his rifle. It
had fallen in the grass and prickly pear close to the trail.
Retrieving it, he walked along the trail to higher ground.

Where was his horse? He remembered it bolting as he
fell, and it might have gotten away, or might be grazing
somewhere nearby.

He followed slowly along the stage tracks. He desperately wanted a drink, but the nearest water he knew of was
at Government Holes, five miles away. And either the at-
tackers or Indians . . .

Or Indians? Now, why had he thought that?

Of course: his gun was still on him, and only the map
was gone. Kurt Wylie then—Wylie, Champion, and Spencer. By this time there might be others, for Wylie might
be working according to some preconceived plan that
Allison's death had interrupted.

They had the map, the stagecoach, and the women.
They would certainly get rid of the stage, for it could only
be a hindrance to them. But the women? Callaghen did
not like to think of that.

He walked on, but when he had gone less than a mile
he pulled up short. A dim trail turned off to the south
through the hills which would lead into a valley beyond, and the stage tracks turned into it. He started to
follow, but his eyes caught a glimpse of something farther
ahead.

He went on only a little way, and saw that the tracks
of the stage returned to the trail. Evidently they had
started to take the trail south, then changed their minds
and turned back. He had gone but a short distance further when he saw the stage.

It was standing alone, with no horses, on the edge of a
small hollow. It was, he knew, standing at Government
Holes.

Taking position behind a Joshua tree, he studied the

situation below him. He could see no one there, but that was what he expected. He felt sure that because of the bloody gash on his skull he had been left for dead.

His head throbbed as he walked slowly down the slight grade toward the stagecoach. Several times he paused in slight cover to study the surrounding hills. There was a point of rocks not far south of the Holes, and a mile or so beyond were the rocks that surrounded Rock Springs.

When he came to the stage he saw that it was empty. Nor was there any blood. Beamis, if he was not alive, had been killed after he left the stage.

Malinda, he recalled, had kept food in a basket under the seat, and he felt for it. The basket of food had been taken, but somebody had left a few slices of bread and ham wrapped in a napkin on the floor under the seat. Evidently one or both of the women had thought someone might come to the coach hunting for food.

There was nothing else of value but a blanket, which he took. The mail pouch under the seat in front was undisturbed. Taking the meat and bread, Callaghen retired to a shallow dip some yards off and ate his small meal.

Returning to the Holes, he took a long drink, and then set out to follow the trail made by the horses.

As he walked he kept glancing at the looming bulk of Table Mountain. From its flat top an observer could see anything moving within miles, but there was no other way to get where he was going. Several times he found spots of shade, and stopped in them.

The wound on his head from what had evidently been a bullet had taken a lot out of him. He had lost blood, and the walking had tired him. He sat down, leaned his head on his arms, his arms resting on his knees. He felt dizzy and sick, and the distance he must cover worried him. What worried him even more was that they should be going north . . . if they were following the map they had taken from him.

He started to get up, but sagged back to the ground, and for a long time he sat there. Then his mind wandered off into a state bordering on delirium.

When his mind cleared it was dark, and there was a soft wind blowing. The sky overhead seemed hazy.

Using the rocks, he pulled himself up. When he felt for his rifle he almost fell. At last he started again, keeping along the dim trail in the darkness.

He was close under the edge of a long ridge that cropped up from the desert, running roughly north and south. If he traveled by daylight he would be visible from the top of Table Mountain. He veered to the west, pointing toward a lower ridge that trailed out from the base of the mesa.

Beyond, somewhere a mile or so away, would be Black Canyon, where the trail down which the horses had gone would go through. For him, without a horse, and with frequent stops to rest, it was almost daybreak before he topped out on the low ridge. Finding a hollow shaded by a boulder and masked by a cedar tree, Callaghen went to sleep.

The sun was two hours high when he awoke, fighting his way to consciousness from a sleep of utter exhaustion. For several minutes he lay still, then he rolled over and sat up.

A wide valley lay before him. Scanning it quickly, he saw a thin trail of smoke against the distant hills. Nearer, almost at the base of the ridge on which he sat, he saw movement. Quickly he took up his rifle and moved closer to the cedar that screened his shelter.

It was a black horse, his horse, moving eastward at a steady walk. He whistled, but he was too far away and the horse did not hear.

Rising, he moved down along the face of the ridge in the direction the horse was taking. Table Mountain loomed above him, and in line with it, two solitary buttes with cedars growing on each.

He walked, ran, almost fell, and reached the bottom not far from the black horse. It was only then that he saw it was following a game trail. There were tracks of deer, and among them the track of a dog or coyote.

He called out, and the black horse stopped, head up, looking toward him. He walked on and the horse moved away warily, then as he continued to talk, it stopped again and whinnied softly.

Callaghen walked up to the horse, his hand out. The black sniffed at the hand, and shied only a little as he took up the reins. "I know there's water up there, boy. Let's go have a drink."

He stepped into the saddle and the black walked forward eagerly.

CHAPTER 20

There were no human tracks around the spring, which lay among the brush and rocks close behind Table Mountain. A butte was near by, one of the twin buttes that line up behind Table Mountain. But there were deer tracks, and several made by a wolf or a coyote—more likely the latter, judging by the size. Callaghen saw badger tracks too, and those of rabbits, ground squirrels, and quail.

He stopped some fifty yards from the spring, with the surrounding area in sight, and spent a good twenty minutes scanning the cliffs and the brush around. At this stage of the game he did not want to lose his hair . . . somewhere Malinda was a prisoner, and if she was to be left alive and free it was up to him.

Beamis, he thought, was probably alive. Callaghen hoped the soldier would make no precipitate move. Champion or Wylie would be quite willing to kill him out of hand . . . if they had not already done so.

After a time he gave in to his horse's impatience and went down to the spring. The black drank beside him, and he refilled the canteen on the saddle.

Squatting on his heels on a high point near the spring, Callaghen studied the country before him. An abrupt mesa lay to the south, gray-black and layered like a cake. East of it there was a gap that was probably Black Canyon. He was riding blind, knowing little about the land that lay ahead. Somewhere south of him Wild Horse Canyon cut off to the west, and that bulk of a mesa might be Wild Horse Mesa, supposedly unexplored.

The ground that lay between him and what he thought

was the mouth of Black Canyon, some four miles distant, was covered with desert plants, and there were frequent hollows. That ground could conceal an army, though it looked innocent and empty. However, there was a thin trail of smoke down there. A cooking fire? An invitation to die? He only knew he must go on.

Back at the spring he drank again, gathered the reins, and mounted. He turned the black, and rode south along the foot of the first butte.

The twin buttes were five or six hundred feet high, with some cedar growing on the summits and flanks. Even where he was riding, they offered some measure of cover. The air was still, and the distant smoke pointed a finger straight into the sky. On the valley floor Callaghen could detect no movement. Several times he drew up, listening, and watching his horse's ears.

He kept on, and came abreast of the second butte. The smoke now lay southwest of him. To the east a mile-wide gap opened into Lanfair Valley. He rode quickly and crossed the gap, then skirting the base of the mountain, he rode toward the smoke. Black Canyon, with its wide gap, lay before him.

Looking toward the smoke, he felt his first doubts. There could be no dodging the probable difficulties ahead. The indications pointed to the Indians being over there. Either they were careless, which he doubted, or they believed themselves safe from attack.

Ridge was dead, and they believed Callaghen dead. Nobody was looking for a stagecoach yet, and the Indians seemed to be far from here, occupied with the army. After all, it was a big desert and there were few Indians.

But why should Wylie and the others be in this area? Did Wylie know something he did not know? Did he have information that was not on the map?

Allison must have told him something to enlist his aid, if that was the way it had come about, and that information might have led them to this place. There were caverns in the rugged mountains to the west, but so far as Callaghen had heard, they were not connected with the legendary caverns that lay under the whole of the eastern Mohave.

In any event, the chase had now come down to a shooting affair, and he was going against three tough men.
Worst of all, in crossing Black Canyon he might be ex-
posing himself, for there was little cover. Callaghen turned
east along the face of the mountain, utilizing whatever
cover he could. He kept his rifle in its scabbard, for nothing picks up and reflects light quicker than a gun barrel.

When he was almost a mile south of where the smoke
showed, he crossed the valley at its narrowest point, coming in behind the ridge. He rode his horse up among the
cedars, finding a cul-de-sac where he could hide him.
There was some grass there, and he picketed the horse.

Not taking a rifle, but only the two handguns, he
started up into the rocks.

It was a weird formation. Here and there it looked as
if great splotches of liquid rocks had been squeezed
from the mountainsides and poured down, only to stiffen
and become hard.

The rock itself was a Swiss cheese of holes. Halting behind an outthrust, he studied the odd formation and could
not decide whether it was volcanic, or whether at some
far distant time there had been a hot spring there, a
geyser that played itself out. He had seen somewhat simi-
lar formations in other lands, where water, with chemicals
in solution, had eaten away at the limestone. In among
the rocks around him, which were of many colors, the
heat was intense. At no place could he see for more than
a few yards.

Apparently there was a sort of passage through the
rock formation. It was not a cave, but a passage open to
the sky, except where rock leaned above him. The floor
of the passage was of sand.

Moving as silently as possible, a pistol close to his
hand, he worked his way through the place.

He had never seen anything like this. The hair on the
back of his neck rose with suspense and dread. It was such
a place as one might imagine to be inhabited by mon-
sters; there was something evil and grotesque about it.

He touched his tongue to his dry lips, and longed for a
swallow of water. Then he could smell smoke . . . wood-
smoke.

He listened, and heard faint voices. He moved ahead cautiously, from one rocky projection to another. The passage had many turns, and the rock was pink or red, and in some places of an odd greenish hue. Just ahead of him the passage branched—one branch seemed to end in an abrupt wall; the other twisted among boulders and offered access to the top.

Hesitating, he heard a sharp *click* and looked up. He could see Spencer standing on the ledge at the top of the rock wall with a rifle pointed straight at him. Callaghen had heard the cocking of the rifle.

He drew and fired, the pistol leaping in his hand even as the rifle belched flame and the bullet clipped rock only inches above his head.

He dived for cover, risking another shot as he moved. A second bullet struck rock near him. Only the fact that Spencer was shooting down at his target and misjudged it had saved him. He felt sure that he himself had scored a miss.

He ran swiftly forward, scrambling up the rocks, gun in hand. He had to get close now, and fast.

He heard startled yells, and somebody was demanding of Spencer what had happened. He heard the answering yell: "It was *Callaghen!*"

"You're crazy!" Wylie called back. "Callaghen's dead—I killed him myself!"

Callaghen ran forward lightly and eased himself between two slabs of rock and up into a corner overlooking a cove in the side of the mountain. From there, on a sandy stretch, a sort of half-moon surrounded by rocks, he could see their camp. He was looking right into it from behind a slab of limestone whose face on his side, was covered with the ripple marks of an ancient sea. On the other side the rock bulged out. Perhaps it had long ago been heaved up from the floor of that prehistoric sea.

He could see Malinda and Aunt Madge, hands and feet tied, sitting against the rock wall. There was a fire, a coffeepot on it, and he could see Beamis a few yards off. He, too, was tied, but he was lying on his face and there was blood on his head.

Champion appeared suddenly, wearing a dirty buckskin coat with fringe, and the same battered hat he always wore. He was a big man, not so tall as broad and powerful. "You set still," he said to Malinda. "I'll be a-comin' back. Kurt may not have much use for you, but I do—the both of you."

Then Spencer came into sight. There was blood on his face. Wylie was with him. "What did you see?" he was demanding.

"I seen Callaghen, I tell you! He was down in a hole back yonder. I drawed a bead on 'im an' when I cocked he looked up. How he got that gun into action so fast I'll never know. I fired, but he shot a shade ahead of me, an' if that durned Spencer didn't kick so much he'd of nailed me!"

"Now talk sense!" Wylie was angry. "You say there's a hole back yonder. Even if Callaghen was alive, how would he get here and get into that hole? I ask you that."

Champion had hunkered down on his heels. "You all better quit your squabblin' an' find 'im. If'n he's hereabouts he surely ain't gone far, an' if'n I know Callaghen he's huntin' scalp right now. Yours an' mine."

"I killed him," Wylie insisted. "I shot him dead."

Champion shrugged. Spencer took a bloody hand away from his head. "If you shot him, he's sure got a lively ghost."

"We should've scouted yonder," Champion said. "I never figured it was anything but a wall of rock an' boulders."

"You never seen anything like it—looks like it'd been burned out by the fires of hell. It's like one great big clinker."

Callaghen eased his position slightly. His firing position was excellent, but to shoot from here would endanger everyone in the camp. His eyes went suddenly to Beamis. Had he seen a movement there?

"Wylie," Spencer said, "we'd better light a shuck."

Wylie shook his head. "No. This is where they said they'd come, and here is where we've got to be. Champ, you're the woodsman. Why don't you go down in there and find out who it was that shot at us?"

Champion chuckled without humor. "Kurt," he said

dryly, "you got plenty o' sand, an' it is surely your idea. I had a look at that hole. You want somethin' down there, you go get it. I wouldn't go into a place like that even if there was nobody down there. I think Spencer saw somethin' move, an' shot. I think he was hit by his own ricochet."

Spencer started to speak, then he merely swore and walked off, dabbing at his head with a torn red neckerchief.

Wylie, six-shooter in hand, went through a cleft in the rocks. He disappeared from sight, but after a few minutes he returned.

"Can't see nothing. That's quite a hole back there—looks like a volcanic blowhole or something. Anyway, if he's down there he can't get out. It must be sixty feet straight down—maybe twice as much. He'd have to have wings to fly out of there."

Champion remained squatted against the rock wall. Callaghen had to smile. The old mountain man had his back to the wall, and he could be seen only from in front. He might not believe all this, but he was taking no chances.

"Who're those folks you're a-waitin' for?" he asked. "How'd they come to know of this place?"

Wylie lit a cigar. "Ever hear of Webb Bolin?"

"That renegade who was in Sonora? Sure, I heard of him."

"He was a stepbrother to Allison, and he has the other map."

Champion looked up. *"Other* map?"

Wylie's smile was not pleasant. "There were two that fitted together, but each was made to look as if it was the whole map. Bolin and Allison got the map from their pa, who spent most of his life down Mexico way. Where he got it nobody knows.

"Somebody, a long time back, spent a lot of time in this country and took out a lot of gold. He also explored a lot, and he claimed there were half a dozen entrances to the cave that he knew of, scattered miles apart. He located two of them—one on each map.

"The story is that he gathered a lot of nuggets. Had

them sacked and ready to take out, but then the Indians located him and he had to fight his way out, leaving most of the gold behind."

"Webb Bolin is comin' here?"

"With two friends of his. They should be here today or tomorrow."

Although the speakers were fifty yards away, Callaghen could hear the conversation easily. Bolin he knew, a thoroughly bad one, known to have robbed churches of their altar services, to have looted homes in Sonora, and to have killed several men. And he had a good idea who would be with him. Bigelow and Barber were two occasional horse thieves, claim jumpers, and worse, who had caused trouble in the gold fields of California and around the silver mines in Nevada.

Whatever he was going to do had better be done before their arrival, but all he wanted to do now was to get Malinda, Aunt Madge, and Beamis free.

Suddenly he realized that Beamis had moved. The soldier still lay on his face, but he was more than a foot from where he had been, judging by the edge of the rock near which he was lying.

Nobody had so much as glanced at him, taking it for granted he was unconscious; but he had edged, ever so slightly toward that rock . . . and closer to the women.

He was not only conscious, but he was alert. Though he was bound, he was obviously thinking of getting himself free and setting the women free; but he could not move much farther without being observed, unless the attention of the men at the fire were distracted.

Spencer had seated himself a dozen yards off and was holding his head in his hand. Callaghen had an idea that he had been badly frightened by his escape from death. Spencer had been a soldier only a short time, and had seen no action that Callaghen knew of.

Beamis needed some help, and he had to give it. Choosing a fist-sized stone, Callaghen hurled it so that it would fall into that deep hole beyond the fire. It flew through the air, struck a rock and rebounded, and fell into the pit.

Wylie turned sharply, drawing as he turned. Spencer

came half to his feet, hand grasping a rifle, but whether to run or to fight it was hard to judge.

"Something moved over there, Champ," Wylie said.

"A rock fell. Maybe it fell by itself." Champion got easily to his feet. "We better take a look."

Both men disappeared among the rocks, and Callaghen, knowing there was very little time, took his long chance. He left the ground, vaulting the natural rock wall and landing lightly on the ground not ten feet from Spencer, whose back was toward him.

The soldier turned sharply around, and as he did so Callaghen took two quick steps and laid a pistol barrel back of his ear. Spencer dropped as if he had been hit with an axe.

Callaghen drew his knife with his left hand and cut through the ropes on Beamis' hands and feet; then he tossed him the knife. "Get the women free," he whispered hoarsely, "and get Spencer's rifle."

Only a minute had passed. Callaghen moved toward the rocks that shielded the descent into the hole.

He heard a foot grate on rock. "Can't see anything," Wylie called out.

Champion did not reply, and it was Champion who worried Callaghen.

Beamis had the rifle, and Malinda and Aunt Madge were moving toward Callaghen. He pointed with his finger to indicate their direction, and stood, gun in hand, facing the opening through which Wylie and Champion had gone.

Beamis moved quickly, his rifle at the ready. For a man who wanted no part of the army, Beamis was doing well. He had the makings of a good soldier. As he closed in behind the women, Callaghen backed after them.

Suddenly Wylie came through the opening. "Spence—" he started to say. He saw the soldier, the women gone. "Champ! Look *out!*"

Then he turned sharply and saw Callaghen. Both men had guns drawn, but Callaghen was ready. As Wylie saw him, Callaghen shot him.

One moment their eyes met. Wylie's gun was in position, his finger tightening on the trigger as Callaghen's bullet struck him.

He buckled at the knees, his head lolling back, then it fell forward as he toppled, dead before he hit the ground.

Callaghen went down the rocks into the hole, bounding from one rock to another.

CHAPTER 21

Behind him he heard a rush of hoofs, and somebody yelled. A bullet struck the rock over his head, showering him with fragments, but he had been only a fleeting, momentary target as he disappeared into the twisting passage with the overhanging rocks.

Malinda was waiting for him. "Are you hit?" she asked breathlessly.

"No." He gestured up toward the place from which they had come. "But there's somebody else up there now. It may be Webb Bolin."

They waited, and Callaghen's breathing returned to normal. Beamis was not in sight ahead of them, but after a few minutes he appeared.

"This hole cuts clear through the mountain," he said. "We're in a trap if they get on the other side of us."

They had no water here, but there was a canteen on Callaghen's horse. "Let's go," he said. He was thinking about a way out, hoping to find an escape route. His pursuers would not know there were two entrances. There was a place where one could see through at the top, but unless they were close to it they could not see it.

"Let's go," he said again in a whisper, and led off, worming his way through the winding passage, flattening himself when necessary over boulders, to reach the far side of the mountain.

Out in the open nothing was in sight except a buzzard circling overhead. Some distance off, opposite the opening, there lifted the massive wall of a mesa . . . Wild Horse Mesa it was called. Ahead of them was Wild Horse Canyon.

"If anything happens to me," Callaghen told Malinda, "try to get up on that mesa, or in the rocks close to it, and stay still."

Mounting both women on the black horse, he led the way along the side of the mountain from which they had come. There were scattered boulders, as well as some cedar and other growth. The greasewood grew in scattered clumps, enough of them to offer a measure of concealment.

He walked swiftly, then changed to a trot. Beamis came along in the rear, constantly looking over his shoulder.

Callaghen kept on, walking and trotting until they had put a mile behind them and were entering the narrower part of Wild Horse Canyon. He glanced back and heard a distant shout, but kept on going.

Beamis came up beside him. The young soldier looked nervously at the rock walls closing in on either side. "They'll have us trapped, Sarge. We won't have a chance."

"It was this or open country," Callaghen said.

Wild Horse Mesa rose seven or eight hundred feet higher than the dim trail they now were following. If they could find a trail up the mesa they might be able to defend it, but he was under no illusions. Bolin and Champion were dangerous men, as were Barber and Bigelow. And there was Spencer.

He slowed to a walk, and they plodded on. Continually, his eyes shifted to left and right.

The mountainside turned and twisted on itself. Its wall might be climbed, but to attempt it here would mean abandoning the horse, and they would likely be caught exposed on the mesa's side. He knew they were in serious trouble. If he could cut back to the south, there was a route that might offer access to the mesa top. He turned and started up through the cedars.

How much farther could they go? Behind them were six tough men, but it was just possible they might give up. Webb Bolin might be more interested in the gold than in eliminating them, and he had not held up the stage, had not kidnapped the women and Beamis. That was Champion's and Spencer's problem.

The climb grew steeper. Ahead of them it led up through scattered cedar. A minor peak was on either side, but possible access to the mesa top was possible between them.

Beamis was some distance behind. "Sergeant," he said, "they're down there—all six of them!"

Callaghen led the horse into a small clump of cedars and tied it with line enough for a little grazing on the rough forage near the trees. Then he helped the women down.

There was no good defensive position here other than the natural outcroppings and scattered rocks and cedars, but it would have to do.

"We might as well settle down," he said when Beamis had joined them. "It looks as if this is where it happens."

"What became of the other man?" Aunt Madge asked. "The Indian who was on the stage with us?"

"He may be dead," Callaghen said, and took a position in a gap between boulders that offered a little shelter. The field of fire was not what he would have wished. "He may have been shot when they attacked the stage."

It was hot and still here. He could see the sun shining on the flanks of the horses down below, saw the men dismounting and tying their horses. They were taking their time, unhurried, unworried.

Callaghen mopped his forehead. This was a long way from Ireland, a long way from the cool, green shores of the Bay of Glandore.

He rested his Henry on the rocks, and waited. Nobody felt like talking.

Major Sykes, with two troops of cavalry, rode out of Camp Cady following the thin line of the Mohave River.

The day was hot, and he kept his command to a walk. The sky was serenely blue, the desert was still. It was sixteen miles to the caves where they would camp for the night.

The hours passed. They made their nooning and then rode on. He had tasted the water of the Mohave and did not care for it, but there was nothing else. The river bed was wide and there were high banks; evidently the river carried, at one time or another, a great volume of water.

Major Sykes squinted against the glare and swore softly. He sat straight in his saddle, however, and carried himself with style. He was autocratic, but no fool; this country worried him.

During a short break when he dismounted the men and gave the horses a brief respite, he spoke to Marriott about it. "There's been a good deal of talk of ambush, but the country seems very open."

"It seems so, sir, but it isn't. There are folds and creases and watercourses everywhere. And this country has been subject to earthquakes . . . they had a bad one at Fort Tejon a few years ago. The worst of it is, our route of travel depends on the water channels."

Sykes was seated on a slab of rock, and Marriott squatted facing him. "Sir, one of my men who served here before says the canyon ahead—Cave Canyon—is tricky. It seems to be all abrupt walls and very high cliffs, but there are ways a man on foot can get down . . . and get away after an attack."

"All right," Sykes said, "let's get a couple of scouts out."

Cave Canyon was about five miles long, and the walls were high, over four hundred feet in some places. They were a kind of conglomerate, and their sheer, fluted sides dwarfed anyone who sheltered in their shade.

There were hiding places, too, in those walls, hollows washed out by water falling from the cliffs, and concealed spots behind the convolutions of the cliffs.

Major Sykes liked nothing about this place, where the walls closed down on them. The men were hot and tired, and did not seem eager to go on. He himself had been glad to swing down and get his feet on the ground.

The volley came out of the lengthening shadows, and the crash of sound cut the stillness, the echoes racketing away down the canyon.

Only an instant, and several shots replied; but Sykes saw nothing that could be called a target. Hastily the horses were led aside, and the men fell into firing positions.

"We've got some wounded, sir," one of the men said. "Two men seriously, three with scratches."

"All right, Corporal—see to their comfort. I think the enemy may have pulled away."

He got up to reach for his canteen and stopped, feeling a chill down his spine. Across the seat of his saddle, from which he had just stepped down, there was a neat groove. A bullet would have cut right through his hips had he stayed in the saddle a moment longer.

For an instant he felt the coldness of fear—actually not the fear of injury so much as the fear of dying disgracefully, or ungallantly.

He did not want to die at all, but if he must die he wanted it to be in a dramatic charge, or even in a last-ditch defense, not shot from his saddle by a sniper's bullet.

"No sense in looking for them," Marriott said. "They'd just fade away in the darkness."

"Double the guard, Marriott," Sykes ordered. "They may make another try."

He was in no mood for conversation as he sat at the mouth of the cave and finished his supper. For the first time he was beginning to see what the warnings meant. It was hard to find an enemy that struck and then vanished. But he might be able to trap them into the open. If they could effect an ambush, so could he.

No enemy appeared, however. Sykes detached four of the men to take a litter and return one of the wounded men to Camp Cady. The other man died during the night.

The twenty miles to Soda Lake was covered without incident, and the next day the march to Point of the Mountain, a further nineteen miles, was equally uneventful until a scout rode in.

"Sir, there's tracks out there—the stage, sir."

"The stage here? But that's impossible. The stage was bound for Vegas."

"Nevertheless, it was the stage, sir. It was accompanied by one rider. I believe it was Sergeant Callaghen."

Callaghen with the stage? How could that be? Sykes's lips tightened with sudden anger. He had deliberately assigned Callaghen to the Sprague patrol to get him away from the stage and from Malinda . . . now he was with it. This could only mean that he had deserted his command to join the stage . . . but why was the stage *here?*

"Are they headed for Marl Springs?"

"It seems so, sir. The rider was leading. I mean his tracks are sometimes wiped out by the stage tracks . . . an' sometimes he rides beside the stage. There's been some trouble on the Vegas road, sir."

"Perhaps," was all that Sykes said.

The command moved out at his signal and he stifled his anger. But it remained within him, a cold, hard knot in his stomach.

Damn the man! Was there no way he could keep them apart? Callaghen was no fit match for Malinda. He was only a common soldier, and Irish into the bargain. She was the daughter of a diplomat, the niece of a general—retired, but nevertheless a general. She had some foolish schoolgirl infatuation for him, no doubt because of those stories that he had once been an officer—if he ever had been.

From their camp tonight they must go on to Marl Springs. There would be a showdown then.

When daylight dawned at Point of the Mountain they had lost three horses and a rifle. The weapon had been stolen from a stack within six feet of a guard, and within a dozen feet of sleeping men.

Noon was scarcely past when Major Sykes led his command around the shoulder of the mountain and into view of the redoubt at Marl Springs. There was no sign of life or movement around the fort until they were within a hundred yards of it, and then the gate opened slowly.

Sergeant MacBrody stood inside, and he saluted as Sykes rode up. "It's good to see you, sir. We've been out of rations for two days."

Sykes rode into the stockade, where three men manned the walls. "Where is Lieutenant Sprague, Sergeant?"

"Dead, sir. He was in bad shape after Sergeant Callaghen brought them back here, but he was killed during an attack after they left . . . shot through the head, sir."

"After who left?"

"The stagecoach, sir. Lieutenant Sprague assigned three men to escort it, hoping they'd get through. There was no food for the lot of us, sir, and it seemed best they make a break for it. I believe they got away, sir."

Four wounded men lay inside the stone house. Sykes turned to Marriott. "Captain, will you see these men are cared for? And unload rations for the others. We'll noon here, and be prepared to move out."

"This evening, sir?"

"We will see. I want the sergeant's report first."

MacBrody detailed the events of the past ten days—the continual sniping, the arrival and departure of the stage, Callaghen's rescue of Sprague's command.

"And you say Lieutenant Sprague assigned him to escort the stage?"

"Yes, sir."

"Were you a witness to that, Sergeant? I mean did you personally hear Sprague give that order?"

"Well, no, sir, I didn't, but everybody knew—"

"I am not interested in what 'everybody knew.' Usually, MacBrody, when everybody knows something it turns out that nobody actually knows anything."

"Yes, sir. It was said, sir, that Lieutenant Sprague, knowing the sergeant's discharge was overdue, wanted him out of it, and Beamis also. He did not believe we had much chance here, sir."

"But Lieutenant Sprague is dead, Sergeant. And we have no direct evidence that Callaghen was ordered anywhere. He may have taken it upon himself to go."

"But sir—"

"Yes?"

"Somebody had to go with the coach, sir. Becker was dead, and Ridge had to handle the horses. The mail and the women had to be guarded."

"I agree." Sykes considered the subject and then asked, "And what about the civilians—Wylie and Champion?"

"They left before, sir. Spencer deserted, and they stole horses and left, sir. I believe they are hunting that mine, the one everybody is talking about—the cave with the river in it."

For half an hour more Sykes questioned the sergeant on every aspect of the events of the past few days. At the end of it he was fairly certain of a few things. The stage

had left, and had gotten away safely . . . as far as those
at Marl Springs could see there had been no attack, nor
had they heard any shots, and in the clear desert air the
sound of shooting would carry for a long distance.

Wylie, Champion, and Spencer had also gone east into
the mountains.

There had been some trouble between Callaghen and
Wylie at Camp Cady, but that might have been staged.
Suppose it was a carefully worked-out plan to escape with
the stage, escape from the army, locate the gold mine . . .

He was being foolish. He must not allow his dislike
of Mort Callaghen to influence his thinking, but the
thought remained, nagging at his mind, which was prepared for suspicion. In any event, he considered the possibility of Sprague sending Callaghen on the stage-guard-
ing mission as unlikely . . . and altogether too opportune.

And who was witness to this? Only MacBrody, another
Irishman, and a friend of Callaghen.

"Tomorrow morning, Marriott," Sykes said, "you will
take C Troop, and I want you to overtake and capture
the stage. I want you to find and apprehend Sergeant
Callaghen—"

"Apprehend, sir?"

"That was the word, Captain. I have reason to believe
that Callaghen followed the stage and Miss Malinda without authority—that, in effect, he is a deserter."

"But the men say he was ordered to accompany it,
Major. Along with Privates Beamis and Stick-Walker,
the Delaware."

"That is correct. That is what the *men* say—all of them
definitely loyal to one of their own. But none of them
actually heard the order given.

"Consider the situation, Captain. A girl in whom Callaghen is obviously interested leaves Camp Cady on a
stage driven by a man friendly to Callaghen. Suddenly
that stage appears at Marl Springs, far off its route, and
Sergeant Callaghen leaves there as escort. I think there is
more than enough reason to believe there is something
more here than meets the eye."

"Yes, sir." Marriott's voice was cool. "And you wish me

to overtake the stage? It may have reached Fort Mohave by now. It may even have gone on to Vegas."

"Find it. And bring Sergeant Callaghen back to me."

"Yes, sir. The stage, too, sir?"

"No, confound it! I've nothing to do with the stage unless it . . . Captain, you may find the stage was somehow involved in this. There has been a good deal of talking about that cave. Callaghen may be using the stage to bring out some gold."

Marriott stepped outside and looked around him. He was thinking that, whatever had happened, there must be a logical and simple explanation. Major Sykes's reasoning was absurd . . . or was it? Had he not known Callaghen, he might have wondered, for it did seem almost too much of a coincidence that the stage should appear at Marl Springs. And how did it happen that Callaghen, who had gone out with Sprague, turned up with a stage that was supposed to be on the Vegas trail? A trail, by the way, that Sprague would not have approached by his assigned route?

MacBrody was watching the men working over their horses. He glanced over his shoulder at Marriott, and saw that as the captain approached he was studying the horses.

"What's been going on, Sergeant?" Marriott asked.

"Hell, sir—just hell. We can't see Indians, but they are out there. Oh, we've killed a few, but mighty few, and we've lost men, too. They'll give up now that you're here. There's too many for them to fight, and it will be too dangerous to try to steal horses. They'll just fade back into the hills and watch their chance."

"Man to man, what do you think of Callaghen?"

"The best, sir. The very best. He's a soldier and a man, first-class both ways. And he's a gentleman—I mean that both as we use the term here and in the old country. If he went with the stage it was because he was told to go, and whatever he is doing it is his duty as he sees it."

"Sprague had it, sir," MacBrody went on. "He was holed up in some rocks near Kessler Peak—that's over east—and he'd never have gotten out if one of his men hadn't brought us word, and Callaghen took them water and led them to a water hole, and then back here.

"In the British army, Captain—and God knows I've no use for them—they'd have decorated him twice over for the work he's done these past several days. Here he's liable to get a court-martial."

MacBrody looked hard at Marriott. "Beggin' the Captain's pardon, sir, and I don't mean to speak disrespectful, but Major Sykes was sweet on the same girl as Callaghen. That Malinda whatever-her-name-is. There'd been trouble between them before this."

Marriott was silent. He had been doing a lot of thinking these past few days. He was an army man, but he was a just man, and he knew a soldier when he saw one. Furthermore, he knew the truth when it was spoken to him like this, and MacBrody was telling it to him straight.

He turned and walked back across the corral. It would soon be night. Somewhere out there in the darkness, there was a stage, two women, and a few men. Somewhere out there were their enemies. He had the rough outline now.

Kurt Wylie he had not liked, spotting him for a rotter right away. Champion was a brute, a mean, dangerous brute. He recalled Spencer only slightly from a previous command as a sullen young man of no particular intelligence. These were the men who were their enemies.

The story of the mine he dismissed. Such stories were told all over the western country. There were lost mines everywhere, and each one was fabulously rich. Maybe a few of them were, but even the best of them wasn't worth even one of the men who died hunting them. That was the pity of it.

Tomorrow he was to overtake and capture the stage, and to apprehend Callaghen. And he felt very strongly that this was something he did not want to do.

The sun was setting and the rugged range that lay to the east was crested with a gold and crimson glow. Deep shadows gathered at the base. What did they call them? The Providence Mountains, someone had said. . . . Well, maybe providence was taking care of those women out there, and of Callaghen too. This was no country for women, but with Callaghen along they had a chance.

The mountain above the redoubt was a glorious color, but now the range across the valley had turned purple . . . an ancient serrated ridge thrust up from the depths of the earth. Had it happened slowly, over untold ages? Or suddenly, in one frightening convulsion? In any case, the winds of the years, the sand and gravel, had done their work on its raw surface.

A man should not stay too long in the desert, he thought, for he could lose his soul to its strange beauty and power. This was where it had begun, and here over countless years nature had been at work. The sun, the cold, the wind and water had slowly changed the rocks, crumbling some, polishing others, and the lichen had eaten at their exposed sides.

This was a strong land, calling for strong men. . . . It was no wonder men looked for lost mines. The more lost they were, the less chance there was of finding them, and so the quest went on, and on, and on.

Marriott slapped his gloves against his thigh, and turned away. He went inside to his coffee, his sparse meal, and a cigar.

CHAPTER 22

Callaghen, waiting between the rocks on the rugged flank of Wild Horse Mesa, had no way of knowing that miles to the north Captain Marriott was leading C Troop toward Government Holes. Nor did he know that Marriott was a man who did not believe in wasting time.

It was eighteen miles from Marl Springs to Government Holes by the Government Road, and Marriott felt that time was now wasting away. If the stage had gone on to Fort Mohave, so much the better; and if it had not, there was the likelihood that the riders of the stage would need help.

Callaghen knew the chips were down. He knew that he was not going on from here, nor was anybody else until the issue had been faced . . . and decided.

The men against him were not just playing games. They had a stake to win, and gold was involved. If there were no witnesses there could be no investigation that would matter. Whatever Champion and Spencer had done would not be known, and what Bolin and his friends found would be their own business, and they would be free to operate as they wished.

Bolin was sure that, whatever there was in the mine, Callaghen knew about it. Hadn't Callaghen had access to the map, and hadn't he been over the country represented on it?

There were two men and two women up there in the rocks. They had very little water and they were not going to move much higher. According to Champion, both men had been doing some shooting; therefore there was not much ammunition left.

164

Nobody could possibly know where they were, and there was no army nearer than Camp Cady, a good eighty miles to the west. But Bolin had run stolen horses through this country a dozen times and he knew where water was, and one place was not two hundred yards from where he was sitting. He held all the cards, and he could wait. They could not.

Moreover, although he preferred not to mention it to the others, he was within half a mile of one of the entrances to what he liked to think of as the Cave of the Golden Sands. The trouble was that that damned Irish soldier up on the side of the mountain was even closer.

Bolin made a trumpet of his hands and called out: "You want to come down, Callaghen? It's no use to shoot each other. Wylie's dead . . . it's just you an' me now."

Callaghen heard him, but made no reply. Bolin wanted to talk, and that meant that Bolin was losing a little patience. It also meant that Callaghen had something Bolin wanted.

Was it the women? It was possible. After all, it was more than a hundred and fifty miles in any direction to where one could find a woman.

Callaghen looked around him. Already shadows were thickening under the mountains to the west. Night was going to be a bad time. Still, under cover of darkness they could perhaps move on up the mesa. He knew, though, that travel at night might be noisy. Loose gravel or rock that one can see in the daytime cannot be seen in the dark. He turned his back on the enemy below and, lying against the rock that was his parapet, he studied the face of the mesa, carefully picking out a possible route.

It could be done, he believed. There was a sort of notch up there . . . it *might* offer access to the top, but then what? Would it be better to fight it out here? No, higher up was better, he decided. Not all the way to the top, but close.

He motioned the others to him and pointed out the way. "Beamis, you'll have to lead. Malinda can follow, as she's a good climber. What we're looking for is water, but what we want most is some kind of a defensive position with a good field of fire. There's too many ways they can flank us here."

"It is too light," Beamis said.

"We'll wait. When it is full dark, you lead off, quietly."

It was already dark down below where the rays of the sun, which had now set behind the mountains, could not reach. Here there was still a half-light. Somewhere he heard the call of a quail, that most beautiful sound of the desert evening.

He waited, scanning the boulders below. He could see the horses occasionally, and for a while there was a thin trail of smoke visible that gradually merged with the night.

"Now, Sergeant?" Beamis asked.

"Now . . . and be very quiet."

Beamis moved out, followed by Malinda. Aunt Madge lingered. "I am worried about McDonald. When I do not come he might start looking."

"Don't worry. You'll be seeing him soon."

She left, and Callaghen listened but he heard no sound. They were moving well, and now he was alone.

He had never minded being alone in the desert. He was not one of those who always had to be talking or sharing thoughts. He liked people, but he felt there was nothing like being alone in the desert or among the mountains, for it is then you begin to know them. The wilderness does not share its secrets with the noisy or the talkative; its secrets come to you with silence.

Animals move, birds stir, and the whisperings of the night become audible. The desert itself speaks, for the earth lives, and in the night's stillness one can hear the earth growing, hear the dying and the borning and the rebirth of many things. A bit of sand trickles, a rock falls, a tree whispers or moans—these are the breathings of the earth.

If there were some way to speed up the sounds of the night, to bring them more precisely to the ear, one would hear the music of the changing earth—the ripples, the falls, the tricklings, all grown into one vast but infinitely delicate symphony that would charm the ear of men.

Callaghen waited only a little longer, and then he drew back from his rock, rifle in his right hand.

"Well, now, you moved just in time!"

A flame stabbed the night just as he threw himself aside and swung with the rifle. It was not a considered blow, merely an instinctive thing with the rifle poorly balanced for it, but his grip was hard as the barrel drove forward.

He felt the burn of flame, and then wild with sudden fear he caught the rifle with both hands and swung, forward and back, with butt and barrel. He heard a grunt, a blast roared from the gun, a choking blast that illumined for an instant a staring face. Then the pistol clattered among the rocks and he swung the rifle butt upward in an uppercut that smashed the man's head back against the rocks.

And then, like a cat, Callaghen was scrambling upward, leaping from rock to rock, ducking the spines of prickly pear by instinct more than by judgment. Behind him a gun roared, and he heard the bullet strike off to his right, but he went between two junipers and on up the slope.

His eyes were accustomed now to the darkness, and he could see to place each foot carefully, wary that he might have a broken leg or twisted ankle should he slip between the rocks. He had no idea who it was he had battled so fiercely among the rocks.

He paused and listened. There was a stirring down there, a muffled curse and a murmur of voices. Somebody struck a light, and Callaghen's bullet spat where the light had been, the sound of the shot racketing down the slope.

He moved instantly, putting himself away from the firing position, and went farther up the slope. He had a feeling they would try nothing more during the night. He had been lucky.

He paused again to catch his breath and heard his heart throbbing, as much from reaction to fear as from the struggling climb.

It had been a narrow escape. Somebody had crept close to him, and in another moment he would have

been dead had he not moved and had the stranger not
felt a compulsion to speak.

Well, he reflected grimly, from the feel of that uppercut butt stroke there was one man who wouldn't be opening his mouth for a while. If the man wasn't dead he
would at least have a broken jaw.

His hand was smarting as sweat got into the powder
burn. He moved up higher, and had climbed for several
minutes when he heard a soft call, barely audible.

"Mort?"

He moved in that direction, and saw that it was Malinda. "We've found a place," she said.

It was a wind-hollowed half-cave in the mountainside,
perhaps thirty feet wide, and less than half that deep,
a poor shelter if a storm came, but a difficult place to
get at. It was a sandy place, partly sheltered by a slight
overhang, and scattered boulders were in front of it, rocks
that had tumbled down the mountain and fallen off the
edge of the overhang, hitting the ground in front of it
to form a not very effective parapet.

"Are you all right?" Malinda asked.

"Yes," he said reassuringly, and Beamis moved over
to him.

"We heard a scuffle down there, and some shots."

"I think one of them is out of it," Callaghen said. "I
don't know which one, but he was a good Injun . . . he
came right up to me without a whisper."

"Champion?"

"I don't think so. He wouldn't have spoken, and had
it been Champion I'd be dead."

"Don't talk like that!" Malinda shuddered and moved
closer to him.

He liked having her close, but not now. A man had
to keep his mind on the business at hand and not be
thinking about a woman at a time like this.

"Get some rest, Beamis," he said. "I'll wake you up
in a couple of hours."

"We can watch," Aunt Madge whispered. "Both of you
need sleep."

Off to the northeast Callaghen could see the flat outline of Table Mountain, low on the horizon, and to the

north the bumpy ridge of the Mid Hills. Due west, not
much over fifteen miles away, was the Marl Springs redoubt. Suddenly he realized he was behind the mountains
at which he had gazed from Mar' Spring.

Then he slept, and in the night he dreamed again
of his battle with Nusir Khan when he and hi wild tribes-
men swept down from the Suleiman Hill: He stirred
restlessly in his sleep, his hand gripping for the sword hilt
that was not there. He awoke suddenly in the gray of
dawn and lay still for a few minutes, trying to figure out
where he was.

He sat up slowly, feeling the stubble of beard on his
jaw, and hating the stiffness of his clothes—the stiffness
of sweat dust and bloodstains. His mouth was dry. He
stared around him.

Only Malinda was awake. There was a faint grayness
along the ridge, a fading of the darkness overhead.

"You were dreaming," she said.

"I've not much to dream about . . . battles and blood
and gunshots. It isn't pleasant."

"No women?"

"Here and there . . . one meets them."

"You've fought a lot?" she asked.

"Most of twenty years . . . ever since I was a youngster
in Ireland."

He turned to look down the slope. It was rocky, and
dotted with cedar and brush. He could see the hind-
quarters of one of the horses, so he knew they were still
down there.

It was a steep drop, some of it a tough scramble, some
of it not too difficult for climbing but there was a lot
of cover, areas where one could not be seen.

Malinda sat close to him. She was wide awake now,
and was not frightened. She had been somewhat condi-
tioned for times like these by the tales her father and
uncles had told; and there had been the time she first
met Callaghen, when he had ridden up out of nowhere,
a dashing and handsome man who had saved them all.

He did not look dashing and handsome now. She smiled
at the thought. His clothing was torn from his scrambles

through brush and rocks, but he looked tough, capable, and confident.

"Do you ever worry about how it will all turn out?"

He shrugged. "A man does what he can, whatever the situation. There's only one way to fight: to win, and anybody who uses force without using it to the utmost is playing the fool.

"I have been fighting all my life, yet I believe in peace. That doesn't do me one bit of good, though, against those men down there, because they have no idea of peace at all. The only thing they understand is violence. They would like for us to go down there and talk peace, but they would kill us all, and that would be an end to it. They would have peace over our dead bodies.

"I have sometimes noticed," Callaghen added grimly, "that the people who preach peace so fervently are doing it from a comfortable place—often after a good meal. It's quite another thing when you face armed men in the night in a lonely place, men who have no standards beyond their own selfish interests."

"I think they are coming," Malinda said. "Something moved down there."

"It's lucky," Callaghen said ironically, "or I'd be needing a pulpit."

He slapped his rifle. "This is one of the best arguments for peace there is. Nobody wants to shoot if somebody is going to shoot back."

He moved the rifle forward a little. "They are coming up the hill because we are in their way. There are only two men, and they believe they can handle us. If there were four of them they would not have even stopped.

"They know Beamis is young, and they know from comments he's made that he didn't want to be a soldier. What they don't know is what a lot of good stuff the young man has in him, and in the last few days it has hardened into real strength."

It was lighter now—light enough for good shooting, and the horses down below were looking up the slope.

Callaghen looked around. On the far side of the hollow there was a space between the side of the mountain and a slab of fallen rock.

"Malinda, see where that goes, will you?" he said.

Callaghen did not like cul-de-sacs. One man could not defend the position they occupied, and if he himself were shot, the others ought to have some kind of escape route. Sooner or later a detachment from Camp Cady would come looking for the vanished stage, but until then there must be some place where they could make a stand.

He watched for any further movement below. He was sure he had put at least one of the men out of action. But he realized that the men who were coming up the slope were not tenderfeet—they were taking their time, sure they had their quarry where they could not escape.

Once he saw a flicker of movement as a man moved into concealment behind a rock, but there was no chance for a shot. It was merely a shadow on the slope that flitted across his vision and was gone.

Malinda was back. "Mort, there is an opening back there. I don't know whether it will be any help to us or not. I doubt if we can get your horse through."

"Does it lead up the slope?"

"Not right away . . . I only went a few yards."

"We'll chance it. You take the horse, and you and Aunt Madge see what you can do. Tie the stirrups up. That might help you get through."

He saw a hat appear alongside a boulder halfway down the slope, but it seemed an obvious attempt to draw his fire and so locate his position. He had no ammunition to waste, and had no intention of responding to such a crude tenderfoot temptation. When he saw something he could identify with some chance of scoring a hit, he would fire.

The sun was up behind Wild Horse Mesa, but his own position was shaded and cool. He located several possible approaches among the scattered boulders and sighted his rifle at those spots so his action, when it became necessary, would be quick and smooth.

It was the right and left flanks that worried him, for the area was too large for Beamis and himself to cover with any success. Their natural parapet was too low to allow them to shift position very much.

He moved over to Beamis. "Take your time, soldier,

and don't waste any shots. You saw where the women took the horse?"

"Yes."

"When the time comes, run for it. Follow the trail until you come up to them. Then try to find another good position."

"You think Major Sykes will send out a patrol?" Beamis asked.

"He will. My guess would be they are marching now. If they can find us, we'll be lucky."

A bullet struck a rock over their heads, showering them with fragments. Hurriedly, they moved to firing positions. Though Bolin was a dangerous man, as were the others, it was Champion who worried him most. The old outlaw was canny, and he could find a route where most men would not dream of looking. Moreover, he was not overly concerned with Callaghen. Whether Callaghen was alive or dead was of no interest to him as long as he stayed out of Bolin's way.

A dozen miles to the north Captain Marriott rode up to the abandoned stage at Government Holes. Only a few miles back they had come on the body of the stage driver, and had buried it in a shallow grave.

The stage itself showed no evidences of Indian attack. Those who had looted it—and little there had been worth taking—had known what to take and where to find it; and there seemed to be no Indian tracks anywhere near.

"It's Wylie," Marriott told himself. Haswell, a stocky Missourian, indicated the moccasin tracks. "Them's Champion's," he said. "I seen 'em around Cady."

Well, then: Champion, Wylie, and whoever else was with them—probably Spencer—had held up and robbed the stage. "A man was down yonder," Haswell said, "and there was some blood. I figure that man is alive."

Marriott could do his own tracking, and he had come to the same conclusion. He was hoping that man was Callaghen . . . if he was alive.

"South?" Haswell puckered his forehead at Marriott's suggestion. "Ain't nothin' off south. I ain't been yonder, but they tell me it's a wild country."

Marriott was wary, but with scouts out, they started south. Haswell rode back after a few miles. "Somebody else follerin' 'em," he said, "and he's poorly off."

"You mean he's been hurt?"

"Yes, sir. I figure he was hurt in that fight, but got away, and then he took after 'em. He's holdin' on, but we better keep a good lookout to right and left. He may crawl offen the trail somewheres."

They found him before an hour had passed, almost at the end of the long western ridge running off from Table Mountain. It was Jason Stick-Walker, the Delaware, and he had been wounded and had lost blood, and had treated and bound up the wound himself.

After a drink of water, and one of whiskey, he told them about the attack, and also said that he had seen the dust of other riders crossing the basin.

"Callaghen's after them. I trailed him to where he crossed this ridge heading south. He was afoot."

Marriott was trotting his troop when they reached the hole in the mountain and the body of Kurt Wylie. "Gun battle," Haswell said. "Wylie had his gun out, but he surely came in second."

"One less," the Delaware said.

CHAPTER 23

Champion hunkered down in the cool shade of a cedar. He dug in his pocket for his tobacco, eyed it critically, then brushing off a few crumbs of dirt, he bit off a sizable chew.

If those damn fools kept climbing up among those rocks, Callaghen was going to kill one or two of them. It made no sense for him to be one of the pursuers. He had suggested a flanking movement, but that was to get off on his own. He trusted his own judgment, but not that of the others.

He looked up at the cliff towering above him. It was almighty steep, but he had a hunch that Callaghen would try for the top. Callaghen was a knowing man, and canny.

Once you knew the kind of man you were hunting, you knew where to look for him. Callaghen would head for the top, and the toppest top around was yonder between those two shoulders of rock. And he would send the womenfolks first, with maybe that kid soldier. He himself would stay behind to stand off Bolin and them.

Champion took another look at the cliff, and started up. What a man wouldn't do for a woman, especially a white woman! They wouldn't last like a squaw would, but for a few weeks he'd have things his own way. He kept on up the cliff.

It took an hour of climbing and scouting to locate them. They had themselves a little hide-out among the cedars and rocks, and the black horse was with them.

He squatted down among the cedars and sized up the situation. No sign of either Beamis or Callaghen . . . which didn't mean they weren't around. From time to

time a shot told him that the ones down below were
still fighting.

Getting off the mesa would be the worst part, but afoot
he could do it. Seemed a shame to leave that fine a
horse, but it might still be here if he came back a few
months from now.

He moved off through the cedars, assured himself that
the men were not around, and then, gun in hand, he
came out of the trees. "Well, now." He spoke in a mod-
erate tone. "Seems like I've found me some womenfolks, alone, and without no ess-cort."

They looked at him from a dozen feet away. Both were
tired, but both were wary, and neither one was frightened.
Got to watch these two, he told himself. They ain't scared,
and they're both thinkin'.

"You gals come thisaway an' come steady. Don't try
nothin' fancy, because if I have to kill one of you I'll
just naturally kill both. You figure iffen you're thinkin'
to make a try, that you might kill your friend as well
as yourself."

Neither one moved. "Come!" he said sharply. "Come
steady!"

They stood still. Both had realized that it was the
thing to do; they doubted he would shoot them where
they stood.

Malinda remembered something Callaghen had once
said to her. "Don't go with anybody who has a gun on
you. A person of criminal mind just wants to get you
away from help where he can do what he wants without
interference. Wherever you are, you are usually safer
than where he would take you."

"I couldn't walk another step," Malinda replied calmly. "I've just climbed all the mountains I am going to.
Besides, I haven't had time to enjoy this place."

He looked at her, admiring her in spite of himself.
She'd be the one to watch. Turn his back and she'd have
a knife in his ribs. He chuckled. "Ma'am, I like your
spunk, but you're surely goin' to walk."

He stepped out and walked toward them. "You walk,
else I'll bat one of you right across the skull."

A moment they hesitated, then started to move. At

that instant Beamis appeared. "Hey! What's this?" He
shouted.

Champion spun and fired from the hip. The rifle bullet hit Beamis and turned him half around, his own shot
going wild.

Champion swung back. The women were gone!

Cursing, he scanned the cedars and rocks with a quick,
overall glance. "You git out here!" he shouted. "Or when
I find you I'll whup the livin' tar out of you!"

The sand told its story. One look at the tracks and he
turned into the brush, swearing as he went.

Suddenly from down the mountain there was a tremendous roar and a crash, and then silence. Dust rose
over the edge of the mesa.

Callaghen heard shooting from the top of the mesa,
two quick shots within seconds of each other. He straightened up, fired two shots downhill, and turning, ran
from the opening into which Beamis had disappeared
some moments before. Through the hole, he turned quickly to see if pursuit was close. His hand touched the wall
and sand trickled from under it.

Glancing up, he saw a huge boulder anchored in the
side of the cliff. The sand had trickled away from beneath
it, and only a few rocks seemed to hold it in place.
Such a boulder could hang so, sometimes for years, until rain or wind supplied the necessary push and down it
came.

Standing back, he smashed at the bank's face, knocking out great chunks of dirt and rock. The boulder gave
a lurch; he started to stab at it again, and jumped back,
barely in time.

The boulder slid a couple of feet, hung a moment
precariously, then fell. Tons of earth and debris followed it. Turning, he ran up the trail.

What had fallen would stop them only for the time
being, and in the meanwhile—

"Hold it!"

He spun sharply around. They were there, three of
them. He had not stopped them at all. By crawling among
the rocks, they had already gotten around him. And they
were boxing him on three sides. There wasn't a chance.

"Private Spencer!" His voice rang with command. "If that man"—he pointed a finger at one of the strangers who stood on his left—"if that man moves a muscle, *kill him!"*

"Yes, sir!" Spencer's rifle came into position.

"Hey! You damn fool!" Barber yelled. "It's *him* we're after! Turn that gun around."

"Private Spencer," Callaghen said, and his voice was cool. "As far as I am concerned, you are not a deserter. You have been on a scout under my orders. Bring this off as you should and I'll see you are made corporal."

"You damn fool!" Bolin shouted to Spencer. "Whose side are you on, anyway?"

Spencer's thinking was slow. He did not like these men very much. He'd had it rougher than in the army, and had been eating less. They'd paid him no mind, and they didn't seem to care very much about him.

Sergeant Callaghen was a man all the soldiers liked. He was a square-shooter—and he'd recommend him for corporal! Spencer had never had any recognition in his twenty-odd years of life, and this was it.

"Yes, sir," he said, "I been on a scout. You sent me."

"Why, you—!"

Bolin's rifle was in his left hand, but at the moment of decision, he went for the pistol. His anger was toward Spencer, but his target should be Callaghen, and in a moment when the greatest concentration was essential he was for an instant without focus. Something struck him hard in the wind as he made his decision, something that struck, and then seared like a branding iron laid across his belly.

Bolin took a step back and stared up at Callaghen, stared right into the bullet that killed him. There was an instant when he saw it there before him . . . knew it for what it was.

There had been other firing too. Callaghen took a step back, and looked.

Barber was down, shot twice through the chest. Spencer was staring at him, dazed, and suddenly aware for the first time of what had happened.

"That was a good job, Spencer," Callaghen said. "You're a good man."

He turned swiftly and ran up the trail and into the cedars.

Champion heard the shooting, prowling among the trees and searching for the women. He'd have them. If that Callaghen would just hold the others off . . .

He stepped for a moment out on high ground with a long view off to the northeast. He could see Table Mountain, he could see . . . It was a column of blue-clad soldiers, riding rapidly toward the head of Wild Horse Canyon.

Soon they would be coming up the mesa. They would have heard the shooting, and they would be coming fast. And there were a lot of men down there—maybe fifty or more.

Champion was not a man who wasted time making up his mind. The mesa was all of three to four miles long and there was a good horse down yonder. If he made it to the end of the mesa, left the horse, and went down the steep side and disappeared into the Providence Mountains yonder they wouldn't have much chance of finding him.

He knew where there was water and a cave or two, and . . . He went for the horse with a rush.

Callaghen came up the slope and saw his horse standing before him. His rifle was empty, and he reached up to slide it into the scabbard when he heard a scramble of feet. Startled, the horse sprang forward, and Callaghen found himself, empty-handed, face to face with Champion.

He did the logical thing. He swung a left to the head and followed it with a plunging dive that knocked Champion back into the cedars.

Champion's rifle was knocked from his grip, and he went down fighting. Both men rolled free and came up fast. This was the sort of thing Champion loved. At a dozen trappers' camps he had never been beaten, at rendezvous and barroom he had been tested, by cattle camp and buffalo pit, he had fought.

He went in swinging, a bear of a man, mostly rawhide and iron by the feel of him.

Callaghen was up and Champion's rush swept him backward. Unable to brace himself, he caught Champion's shoulders and let himself fall, letting the drive of his opponent's lunge carry him on over.

Champion hit hard, but rolled over and came up fighting. Callaghen split his lips with a straight left, but Champion came on in, slugging and clawing for Callaghen's eyes. It was a fight for life. Callaghen went down again, but hooked both hands hard to the face as he hit on his back, then smashed upward with his head to meet Champion's descending face.

Champion stabbed with thumbs for his eyes, and clamped him hard with a scissors-hold on his ribs, slashing with his thumbnails, allowed to grow long for just such a purpose. Callaghen felt a stab of pain as one slashed at his cheek, then threw up his legs and hooked them under Champion's chin, forcing his head back.

He tried to grip Champion's legs to hold them tight so he could break the man's neck, but the mountain man was too old a fighter for that. He suddenly released his grip on Callaghen and rolled back, turning his head slightly to sink his teeth into the calf of Callaghen's leg.

Callaghen let go his hold, and then again both men were on their feet.

Champion was shorter, but much heavier. He wiped the blood from his lips and came in swinging. Callaghen caught him with both fists as he came in, but Champion wasn't even slowed down. Callaghen met him head-on and they stood, toe-to-toe, slugging viciously. Both men were cut, both were bleeding. Callaghen's breath was coming in great gasps, for he had just run up the trail and the fight had caught him unawares.

Champion was grinning. He landed a right in Callaghen's mid-section and Callaghen felt his knees going. Champion took a step back and hit him on the chin. Callaghen went to one knee, and as Champion stepped closer he lunged forward, throwing his right arm around Champion's leg for a single-leg pickup.

Champion's leg was swept high and he fell, coming

down hard into the dust on his shoulder blades. Callaghen backed off, glad of a chance to catch his breath, but as Champion got to his feet Callaghen went in again, ducked under a right swing and, thrusting an arm between Champion's legs, he dumped him again with a fireman's carry, slamming him into the rocks.

Champion got up more slowly this time. For the first time he was aware that this was a fight he might not win. The soldiers would be reaching the rocks, and although the horse was there, he would need a moment's start. He had to get this man, and get him quick and good.

Hands held high to protect his head and face, crouched slightly to offer less of a target, he moved in, and Callaghen feinted. Instantly, Callaghen brought up a whipping right uppercut that snapped Champion's head back hard. A swing with the left to the exposed head, and Champion staggered, almost going down.

Callaghen came in fast, feinting again and kicking the shorter man on the kneecap. Champion started to fall and Callaghen hit him again; but suddenly Champion lunged and Callaghen tried to side-step, but he was not fast enough and Champion's hard head smashed him in the belly.

He felt himself falling, glimpsed Champion stooping for a big rock, and as he hit the ground he rolled over and came to his hands and knees. Champion was lifting the rock over his head, but Callaghen picked up a short, thick chunk of dead cedar and threw it at Champion's face. Unable to duck because of the huge stone he held, he threw it at Callaghen. It fell short, but the flying stick struck him on the arm as Callaghen went in.

He caught Champion with hands down and threw a hard right to the chin. The trapper backed up, blinking, and Callaghen followed, feinted, and hit him in the solar plexus. Champion bent over and Callaghen slammed a knee into his face. He fell forward on hands and knees —and then there were blue-clad soldiers everywhere.

Callaghen backed up and sat down on a rock, gasping for breath.

"Are you all right?"

Callaghen looked up to see Captain Marriott. He started

to rise, but Marriott said, "Sit still. You've done a good job, Sergeant."

He paused a moment. "I have been ordered to place you under arrest."

"Arrest?"

"Yes, Sergeant. Major Sykes is under the impression you deserted your command to join the ladies in their coach. That you coerced them into leaving the route to Vegas, and that you have, in effect, deserted."

"But that's nonsense, Captain. Lieutenant Sprague will tell you—"

"Sprague is dead, Sergeant. He died at Marl Springs. The stage driver is dead, and so are most of his command. I doubt if any of the others will know anything about it."

Callaghen got up slowly. Dizzy from punches, still panting from the fight, he was trying to understand what exactly had happened.

"What about MacBrody?"

"He knows nothing. He understood Sprague had sent you on a scout, from what Sprague had said, and that you located the stage and led it to Marl Springs. He did not actually hear Sprague direct you to accompany the stage as an escort."

"The Delaware knows."

"Good. Although I doubt if Major Sykes will accept his word for it. Both the Delaware and MacBrody are known to be friends of yours."

Captain Marriott put his hand inside his coat. "There is this, of course. It had arrived, and I believe it was to be delivered to you at the earliest possible moment, so I took it upon myself to do so."

His face was expressionless. "You have been a good soldier, Sergeant, and I respect that. From all I have heard, if Sprague were here he would add his word to that. I believe you will have no trouble."

Callaghen glanced at the paper . . . his discharge . . . dated almost three weeks earlier. Allowing for time for it to arrive at Camp Cady . . .

"Thank you, Captain," he said. "Thank you very much."

He started to move away slowly, for he was sore in

every part of his body, and he was only now beginning to realize what a rough go Champion had given him.

Champion, guarded by two soldiers, his face battered and scarred, stood still when he saw him. "Hear you're gettin' out soon. If you ever need a partner . . . say to hunt for a lost mine or somethin', you just call on Champion."

"Sorry." Callaghen shook his head, smiling. "I might have to lick you again, and I'm not sure I could do it."

The desert was still. They saw no Indians on the long ride back to Camp Cady. The air was hot, but it held no malice. They made stops at Rock Springs, at Marl, Soda Lake, and Cave Canyon.

Callaghen nodded toward the walls of Cave Canyon. "There are places back yonder where a man can stand and look up three or four hundred feet. You'd think you were in a cathedral."

The fluted columns were pink, beige, and gray, with darker shadows where the hollows were filled with mystery.

Malinda rode beside him. "Mort, what now?" she asked.

"Why, maybe I'll find a town where they need a marshal, and while doing that job I might study law. You had a point there."

"There's the desert," Malinda said.

"Yes, and I'll wake up in the night and remember it. As it is now, and as it should always be."

"What about the River of Gold?"

"I'll think about it from time to time. I am sure it is there, and I think I know where it is, but when I follow a dream for thirty years like some of these desert rats, there's got to be more at the end than a pot of gold."

The mountains stretched their shadows over the desert, a wind played with the sand on a slope, wearied of it, and let it fall. The Mohave River, along which they rode, from time to time made a ripple over rocks, hurrying onward to its destiny in the Sinks far ahead. There it disappeared in the sand, and reappeared in the dark, silent caverns far underground. Here and there on its way it dropped a few flakes of gold.

"I hope nobody ever finds it," Malinda said. "It should always be there, just to be looked for."

ABOUT THE AUTHOR

Louis L'Amour, born Louis Dearborn L'Amour of French-Irish stock, is a descendant of François René, Vicompte de Chateaubriand, noted French writer, statesman, and epicure. Although Mr. L'Amour claims his writing began as a "spur-of-the-moment thing," prompted by friends who relished his verbal tales of the West, he comes by his talent honestly. A frontiersman by heritage (his grandfather was scalped by the Sioux), and a universal man by experience, Louis L'Amour lives the life of his fictional heroes. Since leaving his native Jamestown, North Dakota, at the age of fifteen, he's been a longshoreman, lumberjack, elephant handler, hay shocker, flume builder, fruit picker, and an officer on tank destroyers during World War II. And he's written four hundred short stories and over fifty books (including a volume of poetry).

Mr. L'Amour has lectured widely, traveled the West thoroughly, studied archaeology, compiled biographies of over one thousand Western gunfighters, and read prodigiously (his library holds more than two thousand volumes). And he's watched thirty-one of his westerns as movies. He's circled the world on a freighter, mined in the West, sailed a dhow on the Red Sea, been shipwrecked in the West Indies, stranded in the Mojave Desert. He's won fifty-one of fifty-nine fights as a professional boxer and pinch-hit for Dorothy Kilgallen when she was on vacation from her column. Since 1816, thirty-three members of his family have been writers. And, he says, "I could sit in the middle of Sunset Boulevard and write with my typewriter on my knees; temperamental I am not."

Mr. L'Amour is re-creating an 1865 Western town, christened Shalako, where the borders of Utah, Arizona, New Mexico, and Colorado meet. Historically authentic from whistle to well, it will be a live, operating town, as well as a movie location and tourist attraction.

Mr. L'Amour now lives in Los Angeles with his wife Kathy, who helps with the enormous amount of research he does for his books. Soon, Mr. L'Amour hopes, the children (Beau and Angelique) will be helping too.